AF615559

I am Virgo

a story by

Tom Allen

I am Virgo
Copyright © 2020 By Tom Allen
All rights reserved
No part of this book may be reproduced in any form by any electronic of mechanical means including information on storage and retrieval systems without permission in writing from the publisher, except by a reviewer who may quote brief passages in review.

Published by Constant Hope Publishing, Aurora Co
A division of Constant Hope LLC

Printed in the USA

My hope is constant in thee!

I am Virgo is a fictional story. All the characters are fictional. Any parallels or similarities to actual events or people is unintentional and completely coincidental.

I am Virgo

Chapter 1

The rain came hammering down, wind driven and pounding on the windows outside Mark Jenkins study. To him, it was comforting. Something about being inside on a stormy afternoon always made him feel good. Sipping his tea, he peered out the window. Even with the weather, it was so peaceful. This was why he moved here. After living in the city for years he had grown tired of it. He was tired of people, telephones, computers, and television, but mostly he was tired of all the congestion. Then, of course, there was all the crime, some of which he helped to solve.

He wasn't a law man. He was an electronic technician who had invested his money wisely in stocks and real estate. He was a smart man, and the police knew it. Sometimes they actually put him on the payroll to help them solve certain crimes, although he didn't need the money. They would give him a bogus title like "Special Officer Jenkins." He didn't mind, he actually liked it, but he was glad to be away from it. Now he could concentrate on other things like his music or perhaps write that book he always said he was going to write. Then again, he had a hard time just keeping a journal.

At forty-two Jenkins was for the most part retired. He spent most of his time getting back to nature and working on his music. Music had always been his passion. He was a singer who taught himself to play guitar. He was familiar with other instruments as well. He had built his own studio in his basement where he would record his original songs.

Mark Jenkins never had time for a wife. But now that he finally did, he wasn't interested in marriage, he was perfectly happy living a stress-free life.

As he drank his tea, he was just beginning to ponder whether he missed solving crimes when he saw what looked like headlights somewhere outside his window across the hills.

About fifteen minutes later there was a knock at his door. He very rarely had visitors and he was not expecting one, especially on an evening such as this. He grabbed his .45 revolver and went to answer the door.

It was the police.

"Mr.
Jenkins?"

"Sheriff Harrington come in" Jenkins was still holding the gun. "You can never be too careful."

"Yeah, I um, know what you mean."

"What brings you way out here on such a nice evening?"

Sheriff Harrington wasn't sure if Jenkins really liked this weather or if he was being sarcastic, "Well I know you don't have a telephone, and you only go to your P.O. box once a week or so, and I needed to get in touch with you *before that*, *because we don't have much* time.

"Can I get you a cup of tea?"

"Yes please, that would be nice."
They made small talk while Jenkins made tea. They didn't really know each other that well. They had hardly ever seen each other, and Jenkins had only been living there for three years. They begin to sip tea....

"Sheriff, what do you mean 'we don't have much time'?"

"Well Mr. Jenkins...."

"Mark"

"Mark, it seems the F.B.I. wants to talk to you."

"F.B.I?"

"That's right."

"As in the Federal Bureau of Investigation?"

"That'd be them, yup. Something about a murder case they're working on. I guess he's a serial killer and they believe he's going to strike again within the next couple of days so they're sending a couple of agents here to Sot Strom and requested your presence. We're supposed to meet up with them inside an hour."

"Where did the F.B.I. get the idea that I could help them?"

"Well, it wasn't their idea."

"Whose idea was it? Yours?"

"It was the killer's."

Chapter 2

The Ecnerwal county four by four was a good tough American made truck complete with big tires, flashing lights, a siren and the word 'Sheriff' written on the side. On the inside were all of the modern conveniences, a couple of pump action shot guns, a cell phone a two-way radio, an am/fm/satellite/cd/mp3, A/C, map lights, cup holders and everything. But even with a good truck, the road was a little bumpy. Apparently, the rain had washed away a lot of the unpaved road.

Mark liked Sheriff Harrington. He had not spent a lot of time with him, but he could tell he was an all right guy. And in fact, he was. The Sheriff was liked by most folks in Sot Strom. The only people he didn't get along with were criminals, and F.B.I. agents. He didn't like people telling him how to do his job, and that was understandable; he did his job just fine, even though there was truly little crime in Sot Strom. Or perhaps he was why. Jim Harrington was well respected. He was in his fifties married for twenty-five and had two grown kids. His daughter was in college and his son worked for a big brokerage firm on Wall Street. Mark Jenkins looked at the Sheriff and wondered if they had anything in common. Jenkins wasn't sure he wanted to be here, here in this truck or here in this situation and he said to Sheriff Harrington, "So what did you mean about it being the killer's idea?"

“Well, it seems the killer left a note on his third victim.”

“Wait a minute, a note? And how do they know it was his third victim?”

“Well, that’s just according to the note.”

“And how do I fit in?”

“Apparently you’re mentioned in the note too.”

“By name?”

“Mark Jenkins. F.B.I. boys think he means you.”

“This doesn’t sound very good.”

“Looks like you might be going back to New York City for a while.”

“Great, just what I need.”

“I didn’t mean to ruin your night, Mark. I’m just doing my job.”

Jenkins thought of the old saying about don’t shoot the messenger. When he realized what song was on the radio, he laughed out loud. The Sheriff looked at him and gave a little smirk.

“Do you like Clapton Sheriff?”

“I suppose I shouldn’t like this song…… but I do.”

Jenkins sang along with the chorus and stared out the windshield into the angry night.

“……. but I did not shoot the deputy………”

Chapter 3

The walk from the truck to the steps of the station house made the two men almost as wet as the walk from Jenkins house to the truck. Their raincoats were nearly useless. Jenkins pondered how even more useless an umbrella would be, especially in this wind. He never liked umbrella's any way.

The station house was a typical small-town cop shop. There was a small entry room where you could shake off the weather and kick the mud off your boots and a staircase going up to the left. To the right was the door the two would go through. There were a few desks and a thigh-high gate. This is where Jenkins met Deputy MacDonald who offered him a cup of coffee. Mark never liked coffee. He had had maybe two or three cups of it in his whole life and disliked it each time. The flavor just didn't do it for him. "Got any tea?" Jenkins asked.

"I'll see what I can do."

Down the hall to the right was a storeroom/locker room complete with bathroom and gun case. Down the hall to the left was the Sheriff's office. And further down in the back were a couple of jail cells.

The sheriff asked the deputy if there were any calls. There were no calls of importance, so the sheriff and Jenkins entered his office. The deputy followed shortly with Jenkins tea.

"Thank you, Deputy."

"No problem Mr. Jenkins"

Mark was not about to tell the twenty-something deputy to call him Mark. For the deputy, "Mr. Jenkins" was fine.

The sheriff said, "Johnny let me know when the *feds get here.*"

"Yes sheriff" and the deputy left the room.

"He's a good kid, a hard worker, known him all his life."

"He seems nice enough" Mark replied.
There was a long pause as the two men settled in and got used to being out of the storm. Sheriff Harrington broke the silence. "So, tell me about you're stint in New York City."

"Well, there's really nothing to tell."

"Just tell me about your life there. Did you grow up there?"

"Sheriff have you ever been to New York City?

"Once on vacation with the wife and kids, you know Empire State Building and what not."

“I didn’t grow up in the city. A lot of times out-of-staters and even upstaters think that Long Island is part of the city. I grew up on eastern Long Island, far from the city. After high school I went to college in the mid-west. I was in my early twenties when I moved to New York City. I was an electronic technician in a large company there, good pay, benefits, the works. I enrolled in the 401k plan and stock options immediately. I was single. Living in a cheap apartment and saving lots of money. I had a friend on wall street....”

“My son Chad works on wall street.” Sheriff Harrington interjected. “I’m sorry. Continue."

“Well, I invested in stock.... got lucky and reinvested.... got lucky again. Soon I had enough money to buy a house. I didn’t have to pay rent anymore and I paid cash for the house, so there was no mortgage. Then I rented out the upstairs apartment. So, I saved enough for another house. I fixed it up and sold it for twice as much. Next thing I know I owned a few houses and a couple of apartment buildings, and I was doing all right. My money kept making money. Then finally I decided I’d had enough of that area. So, I took a retirement package.”

“It must be really nice, retired and so young.”

“I’m adjusting okay, I think. Mind you, the retirement package isn’t enough to retire on, but with my other holdings I should be alright.”

“Tell me about your police involvement.”
“I grew up with a kid named Tommy Boyle. He and I got in a lot of mischief together. He was a smart kid, and funny, but he was always plotting something. Anyway, out of high school he moved right to the city and became a cop. He made detective pretty young, mid-twenties. One night he calls me up out of the blue and says let’s go have a beer. We’re at the bar and he’s telling me about this case he’s working on. I had a few comments., but that was it. A few days later he calls me again, this time just about the case. After that it was like I was a consultant. I helped him solve the case. He told his lieutenant about me and then I became an official consultant. They even paid me. Then I was hooked. I became ‘special officer Jenkins’ but only on the more difficult or bizarre cases. When they would come up, I would go on the payroll for a while. I didn’t need the money it was just a formality to make it official. Then like I said about three years ago I got tired of that area and got out of there.”

“And that’s when you came up here to be with us.”

“That’s right.”

"You've had a very interesting and fulfilling life so far Mr. Jenkins."

Jenkins was little uneasy that the sheriff had stopped calling him Mark. "I can't complain."

There was a long silence. Jenkins finished his tea.

"What do you do up there in that house all day and night by yourself Mark?"

Now Jenkins felt better that the sheriff was calling him Mark again, but he wasn't sure about the line of questions.

"I have a studio in the basement. I do a lot of recording. And I hike and camp in the woods plus I'm trying to write a novel."

"I didn't know you are a musician, and a writer."

"Oh yeah I have always loved music, writing is something I've been wanting to try."

There was a knock at the door and it opened, "Sheriff the F.B.I. gentlemen are here."

"Thanks Johnny."

Chapter 4

The sheriff got up from his desk and he and Jenkins walked out to the reception area. The two agents introduced themselves and they all exchanged pleasantries. Sheriff Harrington said, "Weather getting any better?"

"Well, the rain seems to be letting up but it's still pretty windy." The younger agent replied. Soon the four men were back in the sheriff's office. Agent Fuller was in his forties and seemed to be more in charge. Agent Scott was in his thirties and a little trimmer than agent Fuller. They didn't waste too much time getting down to business. Agent Fuller started: "Mr. Jenkins, you know we have a serious problem in the tri-state area."

"Obviously, that's why we're all here, but I'm not sure exactly what you mean." Jenkins replied.

"There were three murders, one in Connecticut, one in New Jersey, and one in your old stompin' grounds, New York City." Agent Scott produced some photos from an envelope he had been carrying. The pictures showed murder scenes including bodies, chalk lines, and plastic bags marked evidence. In one of the bags was a piece of paper. Jenkins wondered, as he looked at the photos if that was 'the note'. Agent Fuller continued as the sheriff and Jenkins looked at the pictures.

"Now Mr. Jenkins we are reasonably sure that you are not a suspect in any way but, maybe

the sheriff told you, you are connected to this case."
"Yes, something about a note."
"Well, we weren't able to bring the actual note with us, but we made a copy of what it reads." Agent Fuller pulled a piece of paper from his pocket. "We'll be taking you back to New York so you can work with us and the N.Y.P.D. to solve this case. Here's the copy of the note. Why don't you and Sheriff Harrington take some time to look over these items. Deputy MacDonald is supposed to bring us some coffee. We'll give you a few minutes."

This is impossible, Jenkins thought, he couldn't believe what he was reading. Harrington was in deep thought going over the evidence photos. Two men in the same room, with the same information, but totally different perspectives, Harrington was approaching this like a detective. Jenkins was approaching it like a suspect. But the note, that was unbelievable. They both pondered.......

And then Jenkins read it out loud for the third time:

There comes a time in a man's life when he becomes tired of what he is and what he is doing. That's when he joins the other side. Kill as easy as one, two, three. I never knew it could be so much fun. - Mark Jenkins

Chapter 5

In the reception area Agent Fuller was complaining to Agent Scott and Deputy MacDonald about how this weather depressed him and he couldn't wait to get back home to his family.

Deputy MacDonald said, "I don't know if it's el Niño or el Niña or climate change or what the heck it is, but the weather sure has been wacky."

Jenkins and Harrington came into the room. All talking stopped. There was an eerie silence in the station house. Outside the wind and the rain could be heard viciously attacking the building. Agent Scott broke the verbal silence, all the men in the room except him, seem to be pondering life, "We better get going."

"Yeah, it'll be a rough ride to the airport. I hope they can still fly us out of here. The flight is probably delayed because of this fucking storm. We'll check with the radio on the way," said Fuller.

Jenkins, Scott, and Fuller all grabbed their respective coats and attire, then started heading for the door. Just then the lights went out. Fuller grumbled, "fucking storm."
Deputy MacDonald turned on a flashlight and said, "I've been expecting this." The deputy had a flashlight for Sheriff Harrington as well. They all moved toward the front door with the deputy and the sheriff shining the way.

Fuller opened the door and the wind took it a little wider than he had intended. Jenkins heard a pop and saw blood spurt on the wall to his right. He looked at Fuller's face but wasn't sure what was happening. Fuller had a pained and shocked look on his face. Then with another faint pop Fuller's head exploded and his brains decorated the same blood spurted wall while his body just kind of flopped onto the stairs. Agent Scott ran to the doorway and started shooting. Jenkins grabbed the cowering deputy's flashlight at the same time Harrington headed for the doorway to join Scott. Jenkins ran into the back to get two rifles, one for himself and one for the sheriff. He returned to the doorway in time to see Agent Scott's left shoulder explode all over Sheriff Harrington. Jenkins pushed both men away from the door and aimed a rifle in the direction the shots seemed to be coming from. It was a station wagon across the street in the park. While Jenkins was shooting, the car drove out of the dark and into the street heading straight for him. Then the car made a right turn in front of the station house. The driver turned and waved to Jenkins and gave him the thumbs up while pressing the accelerator to the floor. Jenkins blew his brains all over the dash and the car crashed into a utility pole.

Jenkins ran outside to see if there were any more enemy personnel. Harrington wasn't far behind. Mark ran to the station wagon to check for passengers, no, just the dead driver and his

gun. Harrington ran into the park. Jenkins heard someone running up the alley near the cop shop. He ran to the corner to look. No one was there, "Sheriff?" he called out.
"Yeah?" came the reply.

"Anything?"

"....... No...........You?"

"........... No."

Chapter 6

Running back into the station house Jenkins and the sheriff are almost shot by the deputy, but MacDonald fumbled his gun and by the time he had it aimed and ready to shoot he realized who had just run in. This kind of rookie mistake could have gotten him killed if Jenkins and Harrington were the enemy, but they were not, and they were just as glad for his clumsiness. Mark couldn't help the fact that for an instant the line of that song went through his head again (but I did not shoot the deputy).
The sheriff said to Deputy Macdonald, "Call an ambulance."
"I already did they're on their way. I also called over to the State Police for backup."
Fuller was obviously dead, and Jenkins covered what was left of him with a rain poncho, but Agent Scott was still holding on.

Jenkins, Harrington and MacDonald were all in tremendous disbelief. Two F.B.I. agents were shot in their small town right in the station house. The three of them sat there in shock and bewilderment, and maybe a little fear, trying to talk Agent Scott into staying alive until help arrived.
Jenkins said to Harrington, "I want to go outside and check on something."
"What do you want to check?"
"The electric meter."

Harrington told MacDonald to stay inside, and he and Jenkins went out to check the electric meter. When they got out there the storm was still raging and they could see that the electric cable had been cut. Someone had obviously cut it and without getting electrocuted. Someone knew what they were doing. The Sheriff decided to call the other two deputies and have them come in to work.

As they were heading back inside the ambulance was pulling up to the building. The paramedics were looking around at the situation with slight unease as Jenkins and Harrington were still toting rifles. Soon the state police arrived, and the Sheriff told them what happened. Trooper Cazzofaccia and trooper Fodacara assured the Sheriff that they would stay until the other deputies showed up.

The Sheriff had volunteered to take Jenkins to New York City. After Agent Scott was loaded into the ambulance they cleaned up and went back to Jenkins house. The weather was starting to break down to a slight intermittent drizzle. The wind was down to just a breeze. Harrington told Jenkins he would pick him up in the morning to take him to the Lac Clair airport. Jenkins offered the sheriff to sleep over, but Harrington refused. Jenkins went to the fridge and grabbed a beer.

"You want one?"

Harrington said, "Okay but just one."

Jenkins cracked them open and handed one to Harrington. They both took a sip.

Harrington said, "I've seen this around but never tried it, it's good."

Jenkins replied, “Yeah Black Forest is my favorite.” They sat down and enjoyed their beer. There was no talking. After Harrington left, Jenkins repacked a bag, took a shower and then got a few hours of sleep.

The ride to the airport was about an hour, and the flight to New York would be about an hour and a half. Out on route 21, the inside of the county four by four was quiet. Finally, Sheriff Harrington broke the silence, “You could have been killed last night.” He said to Jenkins.

Mark looked at Jim Harrington and wondered if the sheriff had ever seen as much action in all his years on the job as he did that night. Then he responded, “You too.” Both men were still a little shaken.

“Mark, why did you push us out of the way like that?”

“I saw that agents arm just about get blown off sheriff and a lot of his shoulder was all over you. Neither one of you was in any condition to be shooting back at that asshole. And I knew with the rifle I had a better chance of hitting the target.” Jenkins replied.

“You did a lot of quick thinking. You probably saved my life.”

“I just did what I had to do Sheriff, but you’re welcome.”

“Where’d you learn to shoot like that?”

“I’ve had a passion for guns ever since my Dad bought my brother and I a bb gun when I was about nine or ten. But with that wind and rain last night I have to believe a lot of it was luck. "

Sheriff Harrington thought for a moment as if still trying to digest the shootout. "It's been a long time since I was in a shootout."

"Yeah, I was wondering about that." Mark could see the sheriff wasn't going to offer any more at that time so they both left it at that. The inside of the county four by four fell silent again.

Route 21 was very scenic with great views of the Adirondacks. Jenkins always appreciated their beauty. It was not raining, the sun was out and visibility was good, although it was still pretty windy. Jenkins was trying not to think about what was ahead, and instead he was just enjoying the scenery. They were near an open field and the wind was blowing the county four by four pretty hard. Harrington said, "I hope this plane is flying today."

Chapter 7

Arriving at the airport, Jenkins thought to himself that this is only the beginning. What kind of nightmare was he in the middle of? He also knew that things could only get worse, before they got better, if they ever got better again. He decided he was going to make the best of it.

The Lac Clair airport was very small. Commercially the largest plane that flew out of Lac Clair was a Cessna 402, but the runways were long enough to accommodate small jets. The feds had arranged to have a Gulfstream SPX there to take the men to LaGuardia airport in New York City.

They met the pilot and copilot in the small waiting area at the small airport terminal. The weather seemed to be a little calmer than it was when they were in Sot Strom. The pilot assured them that they would be flying. Moments later they were on the plane and in the air.

Jenkins was deep in thought as he stared out the window over the Adirondacks. A part of him did not want anything to do with any of this, but another part of him liked it a lot. That was the part of him that scared him. And it was the part that Tommy Boyle would understand.

Harrington on the other hand wanted nothing to do with it. He'd already seen and known too much. He just wanted to get Jenkins to the NYC authorities and head back home. Maybe he'd go see his son Chad while he was there, have dinner with him or something. Lost in thought, he was snapped out of it by the plane descending and, in the process, hitting air pockets. He did not like to fly, especially these small planes. The pilot had told them it might be a little bumpy on the way down, and it was. And both men were relieved when the plane was finally on the ground.

Brad Tolliver was sitting at a desk talking on a phone. He never did trim his hair after his time in narcotics and kept it in a ponytail and out of sight. "I think it's one of those small jets, a Gulfstream or whatever" his New York accent was evident. On the other end of the phone conversation Tim Ford was telling Brad Tolliver that he thinks the plane just landed. "Bring him straight here." Tolliver said. The voice through the little phone speaker was protesting, "But the feds said that w…."

"Fuck the feds bring him here!" The conversation was over.

Duncan Vestapool was sitting on a chair across from where Tolliver was sitting. "How well do you know this guy?"

"Well, enough to predict that he can be a big help in solving this case" Tolliver said dropping a folder on the desk.

It was obvious that Vestapool had reservations.

"He's an old friend. Don't worry about it."

Tolliver knew that in order to get to the meat of a case you had to immerse yourself in it. He knew that Mark Jenkins would do that. That's how Jenkins always was. Brad would try to work many cases at once, but Mark was only recruited to work on one at a time. Sometimes Jenkins would study a case for hours a day, for a week or two then he'd have the answer. Tolliver knew it was a good idea to have Jenkins involved but he wished the situation wasn't so sticky with Jenkins name being directly involved and named in the note.

Then Vestapool said. "What if he's our guy?"

Tolliver looked a Vestapool. Vestapool thought that look would kill him if he hadn't left the room.

Brad Tolliver picked up the phone, "get me Tommy Boyle, right away."

Tommy Boyle was a rare kind of cop, the kind that people like. He wasn't pretentious or stuck up like most cops. He didn't consider himself above the law, like most cops do. He would never break the law like most cops did. He just wanted to help people, to serve and protect. Lieutenant Tommy Boyle was a good guy, who probably could have done better in a different *field, but this is what he was – a cop.*

The phone rang. He let it ring again. He knew things were about to get crazy. Finally, on the fourth ring Boyle answered the phone. He looked into his cup of coffee and thought about how Jenkins never liked coffee. After a few seconds he said into the phone, "On my way."

Chapter 8

Jenkins was looking through the window of an airport gift shop while he waited for Harrington to come out of the men's room. He had a fleeting thought of fleeting. In the window he saw "gifts" that made him wonder why. There were large gaudy earrings, shot glasses, bookmarks, and other crap. There were also New York fridge magnets some even said, "Niagara Falls." Niagara was hundreds of miles from where Jenkins was standing. Did people actually buy this shit? Perhaps people on business trips promised to bring their children something back but found themselves at the airport when they remembered and had to pick up some crap at this gift shop. Just as he started to wonder why he cared; he could see in the reflection of the window that Harrington was walking toward him.

"Bet a part of you thought I'd be gone."

"Nope, not at all, but I bet you thought about leaving."

"Briefly"

"Okay Mark, we have to find the baggage claim that's where they want to meet us."

"It's this way Sheriff, follow me."

Detective Tim Ford met Sheriff Harington and Mark Jenkins near the baggage claim. The Sheriff had to sign a release then his responsibility for Jenkins was finished. He signed the form and he and the detective talked briefly. Jenkins put out his hand and the

Sheriff took it with a smile and said, “Thanks for saving my life.”
“You’re welcome.”
“Perhaps I will see you again when you’re done here.”
“Perhaps. Have a safe trip back.”
With that the Sheriff left, and Jenkins was left with Detective Tim Ford who said, “Mr. Jenkins please follow me.”
“I’m right behind you.”

Brad Tolliver was waiting. He was thinking about when he met Jenkins all those years ago at Tommy Boyle's house. They hit it off right away. Tolliver admired Jenkins and enjoyed his company. It will be good to see him again.

Ford pulled the Chevy up to the curb. Jenkins knew this building. He'd been here many times. He didn't think he'd enjoy coming back for a visit, but he was kind of excited and more than a little anxious. Then he saw a face *he recognized and moved straight toward* Tommy Boyle.

"Hey Tommy! Good to see you again man!"

"Mark, how are you?" The two men embraced.

"I'm good."

"Let's head right upstairs."

Jenkins ignored the fact that Tim Ford was no longer with them.

"Mark, we have to go up and see Captain Tolliver."

"Wait, Captain Brad Tolliver?"

"That's who we're going up to see."

"Oh, so Brad made Captain. I thought we were heading up to your desk."

"My office is no longer in this building. Listen I'm glad you are here, not only to help us with this case but to help us clear your name too."

Jenkins just looked at Boyle and the left side of Jenkins closed mouth rose up in an upward curl giving a half smile. They went inside.

Chapter 9

Trooper Cazzofaccia was sitting at a desk in the Sot Strom cop shop talking on the phone with an FBI agent. Trooper Fodacara and Deputy MacDonald were there with him. Occasionally, he would look up at MacDonald, cover the mouthpiece of the phone and ask the Deputy a question, just to make sure he was getting the story straight for the feds.

"...Yes, they flew out this morning............okay .... bye"

Deputy Stevens and Deputy Harris had just been sent home. They had been up all night with the troopers guarding the cop shop while MacDonald went home and got some rest. Cazzofaccia hung up the phone and once more he and Deputy MacDonald went over the previous evening's events in detail for the official report. A federal officer had been killed in the line of duty and they knew that the report had to be well written. MacDonald was still shaken by what had happened. He had definitely not ever seen anything like it before. As such, he was able to recall it in vivid detail. The nearest Crime Scene Investigators were in Albany and they were on their way up. The doorway to the cop shop was left pretty much the way it had been the night before. Most of Agent fuller's remains had been removed by the coroner but some of his brain matter and skull bits were still on the wall and floor. They

were not to clean it up until after CSI had done their work.
Cazzofaccia looked at MacDonald, "Did you hear from CS yet?"
"Not since they left Albany" said the deputy, "I can't believe they are on their way up here. A few years ago, we had a young boy get murdered and they didn't show up for days."
"That may be one of the reasons they are on their way up here." said Cazzofaccia, "That and the fact that a fed was killed."
"Yeah, I'm leaning more toward the fed." said Fodacara.

The station wagon was still outside roped off and covered with a tarp. The driver's remains had been removed also except for spatter, brain and skull bits. CSI would have to investigate that too. It was all very surreal to a small town in which the biggest crime was disorderly conduct and traffic violations, not counting the boy that was murdered in his home which Macdonald had mentioned. Two people being killed in a police shootout and one of them being a fed, that was big news. And of course, it was the talk of the town as would be the case in most small towns.

MacDonald answered a ringing phone. "Oh, Hey Sherriff....... Yup the troopers are still here. .... We're waiting on CSI to come up from Albany....... Okay Sherriff see you tomorrow."

Trooper Cazzofaccia stood up, "I'm going back outside to look at that wagon." Fodacara followed him out.

Deputy MacDonald finally had some time to himself. He was still a little shocked from all the recent activity. Sot Strom was a quiet mountain town and rarely did anything of any magnitude happen there. He poured himself a cup of coffee and started reading over his report of events. He wished the Sheriff was there to look it over. He always felt better when Sheriff Harrington was around anyway. He wondered if there were other killers on the loose in the *area. He doubted that the dead guy in the* station wagon was the only perpetrator. He had to stop letting his mind wander and concentrate on getting his story straight while it was fresh in his head.

Outside, the station wagon was cordoned off with crime scene tape and rope. The body had been removed by the county coroner. The driver's door was open and covered with a blue tarp. Trooper Cazzofaccia and Trooper Fodacara took off the tarp and were looking at the inside of the station wagon.

Deputy MacDonald walked to the doorway of the cop shop to watch them. He was wondering if they should be touching it at all, let alone poking around like they were. After a while, the two troopers head back into the cop shop.

"The Sherriff says he's staying in New York City tonight and returning tomorrow." MacDonald told the troopers.

"I guess that leaves you in charge." said trooper Fodacara, "we've done all we can do for now. Call us when the crime scene people get here."

"Okay." said MacDonald, and the troopers left.

For the next few hours Deputy MacDonald was left alone in the cop shop taking a few calls. One loose dog, one domestic dispute, and one fender bender. MacDonald couldn't leave the cop shop, so he had to call in Deputy Harris to go check out the fender bender. Soon after he hung up from Harris, the crime scene people arrived.

"Hi, I'm Gloria Grundle, Crime Scene. I'm a forensic investigator, this is my partner Bob Miller, he's a crime scene analyst." said the female CSI.

"I'm Johnny MacDonald, I'm a Deputy here in Sot Strom."

"Nice to meet you, Deputy. Can you fill us in on what happened here?" Said Bob Miller

The deputy proceeded to tell them everything that happened. As they were listening, they were studying the doorway area of the cop shop. Then they asked him to continue his story while he followed them out to the station wagon. When the deputy finished the story Grundle said, "Looks like this scene has been compromised." The deputy didn't say anything. But Miller agreed with her. Then the deputy told them he had to make a phone call and he called the Troopers to let them know

CSI had arrived. Soon after as Grundle and Miller were studying the scene and taking samples and pictures, the troopers arrived.

Trooper Fodacara spoke first. “I’m Fodacara and this is Cazzofaccia.” the CSI’s laughed before introducing themselves. “What’s so funny?” Said Cazzofaccia.

“Interesting names” was Miller’s reply.

“Yeah, so did the deputy fill you in?” asked Fodacara.

“Pretty much” answered Grundle.

“We were checking out the wagon earlier.”

Grundle said, “Oh, so you’re probably the idiots that compromised our crime scene.”

Cazzofaccia was visibly upset, “Hey what’s your problem?”

“No problem, Officer,” said Miller, “but we do have work to do.”

With that the troopers went into the cop shop, but Grundle called after them, “Hey try not to compromise the doorway if you don’t mind.”

The two troopers were not happy with the attitude of the two CSIs, but they realized there wasn’t much they could do about it. This was very frustrating to them. If it was just about anyone else, they could arrest them and give them an attitude adjustment. They knew that wouldn’t fly in this situation.

“Some fucking attitude out there.”

“Yeah, we have to let it go.”

“Hey MacDonald, we’re going back to Jay Brook. Let us know if you need us for anything else.”

“Okay, but we should be fine. The Sherriff will be back in tomorrow.” MacDonald replied. After about an hour the CSIs came in and asked MacDonald where they could set up shop. He led them to a back room which was not being used. Then they asked if there was a motel in town. The deputy gave them directions to the motel and gave them the telephone number and the owners name.

A couple of hours later the CSIs went to the motel and MacDonald was relieved by Deputy Stevens.

Chapter 10

As Mark Jenkins and Tommy Boyle were heading up the stairs someone coming down the stairs said, “Good morning, Lieutenant.” to Tommy.

“Good morning,” Boyle returned.

Then Jenkins said, “Lieutenant?”

“Yeah, didn’t I mention that?”

“No, but I should have guessed it.”

They arrived on the third floor and started walking down the hall. Coming toward them was a detective. He said “ah so this must be the famous Mark Jenkins, are you sure you’re heading in the right direction Lieutenant? Lock up is downstairs.”

Boyle said, “Go get me some coffee, Vestapool.”

“Yes sir, Lieutenant.”

Jenkins started to feel a little uncomfortable. Tommy could sense his unease, “don’t listen to him. He’s just an asshole cop. Like most are.” Jenkins said, “You’re a cop.” and Boyle replied, “Guess I’m an asshole too.” That’s when they arrived at the door marked Capt. Tolliver. Boyle knocked on the door, and they were invited in. “Mark, it’s great to see you!” Said Captain Brad Tolliver as he made his way around his desk to embrace Jenkins. “Great to see you too, Brad!”

The three settled in and soon Vestapool brought them coffee. It was obvious that

Vestapool had an attitude directed at Jenkins. Captain Tolliver brought Detective Vestapool down the hall to straighten him out. After that Vestapool was polite to Jenkins, but it was obviously painful for him.

Tolliver closed the door so that he, Boyle and Jenkins could have some privacy. They started talking about old times. After sharing a few laughs, they got down to business. First off, the two cops wanted to know about the shooting in Sot Strom. So, Jenkins filled them in on what happened at the Sot Strom cop shop. "Wow, you saved that Sheriff's life." Said Boyle. "You always were a good shot."

Boyle and Tolliver then started to fill in Jenkins on the murders. Tolliver was explaining that he was under a lot of pressure from the feds now to find out what was going on and to prove Mark Jenkins is innocent. Just when they were getting to the details of the murders Tolliver's desk phone rang and someone was knocking at the door at the same time. Tolliver turned the ringer off the phone, "come in!"

It was Tim Ford. "Another body's been found sir."

"Thanks Timmy"

Tolliver picked up the phone. "Yeah, I just heard... I'm on my way."

Chapter 11

Sheriff Harrington had taken a cab from LaGuardia airport to Manhattan. He was on his way down to check into a hotel down in the financial district when his cell phone rang. It was his son Chad. Father and son finalized the plan for getting together that evening and then the Sheriff paid the cabbie.

The Wall Street Inn is a small but nice hotel near the southern tip of Manhattan. Harrington had stayed there before, and the price was comparatively reasonable. After he was checked in and after a nap the Sheriff headed out to have a beer. He decided to walk down to Fraunces Tavern. He liked the historical aspect of the tavern. It had been there since 1762 and George Washington said goodbye to his officers in the building. Harrington was enjoying a Porterhouse Red draft and took out his credit card from his wallet and noticed something stuck to the outside of his wallet that he didn't recognize. It was a small sticky note that read "101 Willoughby, tomorrow 3pm. Signed V." He looked at the note front and back it was a little disturbing. How did it get on his wallet and when and who?

Harrington sat at Fraunces Tavern sipping his Porterhouse Red Ale wondering what he should do about this sticky note if anything. Then he decided to text Jenkins to see what he thought. Maybe Jenkins put it on his wallet as a joke. But that wouldn't really make sense considering the seriousness of the events of the past night. Who is V? So, he texted Jenkins - "found a sticky note on my wallet. Give me a shout." He put his cell phone away and decided that he was enjoying his ale so much he would have Chad meet him at the tavern.

Tommy Boyle, Brad Tolliver, Tim Ford and Mark Jenkins were on a sidewalk in Manhattan with a couple of other police officers and a couple of FBI agents. About 10 feet away from Jenkins was a body. The victim was a male.
"This is a change in pattern," said Boyle.
"But the puncture wounds are similar" was Tolliver's reply.
Boyle, "same weapon?"
Tolliver, "maybe."
Detective Lucy York came over to the group and said, "Crime scene just arrived."
Boyle said, "Thanks Lucy."
The CSI's asked for some room and started looking over the scene and taking photos. Then they checked the body and took photos of it. Then they searched the pockets of the victim for evidence. They found a plastic bag in a pocket and in the plastic bag was another note. Jenkins immediately began to hope that his name was not on that note.

About that time Jenkins got a text from Sherriff Harington. Jenkins called Harrington. Harrington took the call outside of Fraunces Tavern.
"Mark, I found a sticky note on my wallet."
"What did it say?"
"101 Willoughby, tomorrow 3pm. Signed V."
While Jenkins was listening to what Harrington was saying, he could also hear the CSI reading the note found on the victim. The note said: "I am V."

Tommy Boyle saw the look on Mark's face and asked him what was going on. Mark continued talking to Harrington and told the Sherriff that they may need him to bring the note up to the precinct. The Sherriff agreed to bring it up the next day. Mark hung up the phone and told Boyle that Harrington got a note that could be a connection and he's bringing it to the precinct tomorrow.

Back at the precinct, Tommy Boyle offered to give Jenkins a ride to the hotel that the NYPD were putting Jenkins up at. Jenkins took the ride. They pulled up to the Woodcalling Hotel on 35th and Jenkins was not impressed. Tommy said: "Hey sorry, I know it's not the best but it's all the department will afford."
"It will do" Jenkins replied, "I'm just glad the department is not putting me up at the ole grey bar." They both laughed. "I'll be alright, thanks for the lift, see you in the morning."

Jenkins went in to the less than par hotel and checked in. He got to his room and set up a small electronic device on his room phone. Then he dialed something on one of his two cell phones and head out with his bag, which he had not unpacked. He decided to check in to the Ritz Carlton under his pen name Allen Thomas. After all, why should he stay at a sub-par hotel when he can afford much better. He didn't want to hurt Tommy's feelings, so he just let Tommy think he was staying at the Woodcalling. If Tommy or anyone called the hotel room phone it would be forwarded to his cell phone thanks to the device he installed on the phone at the Woodcalling.

Mark finally settled into his room at the Ritz, had a bath and prepared to have a great night's sleep. He remembered being poor and didn't like it. Staying at the Ritz made him feel that all was right with the world, even if the world said it wasn't.

Chapter 12

The next day Jenkins woke up at 8 AM feeling refreshed after having had a great sleep. His meeting at the precinct wasn't until 10 AM. His cell phone which was patched through his room at the Woodcalling started to ring.

"Hello?"

"Hey, just making sure you are up. You want me to send someone over to get you?"

"Hey Brad, yeah, I'm up. No thanks I can make it over there myself. It's only a couple of blocks. Ten o'clock, right?"

"Yeah, See you at 10."

"Okay see you then."

As Jenkins pushed the button that ended the call, he started to feel uneasy again. He was thankful for the night of luxury in his room. He had booked the room for a week, so he knew he was going to be back tonight and that was a comforting thought. But he was thinking about this serial murder case and how it may mean some unpleasant business over the next few days or even weeks. He did enjoy hanging out with his old friend Tommy Boyle again though.

He took his time getting ready and by 9 he was out the door. When he got to the conference room on the third floor of the precinct building Sherriff Harington was already there. Jenkins went over to greet him.

"Hello Sherriff"
"Hey Mark, long time no see."
"Did you connect with your son Chad last night?"
"Yes, we had a nice time. How was your night?" Harrington asked.
"It was fine. I slept well; I think I needed it."
"I'm sure you did. I think we both did."
The two men went on to talk about the note that Harrington had found stuck to his wallet and the note that was on the body found the day before. Jenkins asked to see the note. Harrington pulled it out of a large envelope he was carrying. He had placed it in a plastic bag. While Jenkins was looking over the note and he and Harrington were talking, the room began to fill up.

They took their seats around a large conference table. Mark Jenkins, Sherriff Jim Harrington of Sot Strom NY, Lieutenant Tommy Boyle NYPD, Agent Don Holzer FBI, Agent Jeff Bullis FBI, Agent Carol Foster FBI, Captain Brad Tolliver NYPD, Detective Tim Ford NYPD, Detective Duncan Vestapool NYPD, and Detective Lucy York NYPD were all seated, and the conversation began. Brad Tolliver opened it up.

"Good morning everyone. I know it's not the norm to have a group like this gathered for a meeting, but our situation is not normal either. There is a serial killer out there who is changing his or her modus operandi and piling up bodies quickly. All of us at this table must work together and solve this case as soon as we can. The FBI has agreed to work with us and to share jurisdiction and resources. I'm hoping that together we can end this before it gets even more out of hand."

Tolliver started laying out the evidence from the case on the table. Jenkins looked at Agent Don Holzer and said, "Any word on how Agent Scott is doing?"

Agent Holzer replied, "He lost his arm, but he's *alive*."

They all started looking over the evidence. Jenkins had seen most of it or copies of it when he was in the Sot Strom cop shop, but now it seemed much more real to him. Tolliver turned on a projector and asked detective Lucy York to take over. Jenkins knew York. He and she had been romantically involved a few years back. As Jenkins watched her, he still found her incredibly attractive. He wondered if she was still angry at him.

York started her presentation/slide show. "The first body was found in Washington Square Park. Victim was a white woman in her late 20s, Elaine Shoeman blond hair blue eyes a student at the fashion institute. Multiple stab wounds on her body and one to the left eye. The coroner found a Maple leaf stuffed into her mouth. Sugar maple to be more precise.

The next body was found in Weehawken, New Jersey close to the Lincoln Tunnel. The victim was a white woman in her early 30s Jane Tyson, dark hair brown eyes similar stab wounds as Elaine Shoeman, except no puncture to the eye. The coroner found an oak leaf, red oak, stuffed into her mouth.

The third body was found just outside of Greenwich, Connecticut. The victim was a black woman in her late 40s, Tameka Wilson. She had similar stab wounds except most of her wounds were in the back. The coroner found an oak leaf in her mouth, white oak. A note was found on her person that mentioned Mr. Jenkins" as Lucy York said this she gestured toward Mark. Surprisingly, it didn't really make him uncomfortable. She continued.

"The fourth body was found yesterday in Cortlandt Alley, Tribeca. The victim was a white male in his late 30s John Beckford. He had similar stab wounds as the other victims indicating that the same or a similar weapon was used. No leaf was found. He also had a note on his person. The note read simply - 'I am V.'"

Lucy York had finished her presentation/slide show and sat down. Tolliver picked up the conversation again. "The only thing I want to add is that Sherriff Harrington found a post-note on his wallet that said '101 Willoughby, tomorrow 3pm. Signed V.' That was about the same time that we found the note on Beckford. It's kind of scary and a little creepy that this guy could have gotten that close to Sherriff Harrington, nevertheless, I think we should take it seriously. Since we must assume the note was written about today, I will have the building watched and I'll take a detail over to Brooklyn to be there by 3. In the meantime, we need to brainstorm. Work together in whatever groups you are comfortable with and share information, hunches, and evidence. We have a much better shot at stopping this killer if we all work together. Sherriff Harrington, thanks for your help. I assume you'll be heading back up north."

"Yes, that's the plan."

"As for the rest of you if we don't talk by tomorrow then we'll all meet again right here same time."

On the way out of the conference room Jenkins caught up to Lucy York. "You still angry?"

"Yes, but not like I was."

Chapter 13

Brad Tolliver's office smelled like a mix of coffee, hand sanitizer and tuna fish. Except for the shuffling of papers there was no sound. Tolliver sat at his desk while Jenkins and Boyle sat at the table.

Tolliver broke the silence, "Mark what have you figured about the note with your name on it?"

Well, I haven't come up with anything concrete. I thought maybe someone trying to get payback. Perhaps a relative or friend of someone I helped you guys put away. Then I thought maybe the killer passively knew me. And I also thought...."

"What?" Said Boyle, "Inside job? Possibly a police officer with a grudge?"

"Well... yeah."

"We thought of all that too." assured Tolliver. "But that doesn't really narrow it down the way we'd like it to."

"What about the weapon?" Jenkins asked, "Do we know anything about that?"

"We know its smooth, sharp and sort of cone shaped," Said Tolliver. "The coroner found no traces of wood or metal or anything else."

Jenkins thought for a moment, "Could it be some kind of stone or quartz or even glass?"

“We’re not sure yet, but we need to work on that. If we figure out what the weapon is, we may be a lot closer.” was Boyles answer.

Jenkins was going down the list in his head, “What do we know about the victims, any common thread?”

Boyle said, “We’re just starting to get the info on the victims. We haven’t been able to compare it yet.”

Tolliver got up from his chair, “I guess we don’t really have much to go on just yet. Tommy maybe after lunch you can grab a couple of guys and we’ll all go over to Brooklyn to see what happens at 3.”

Boyle replied in partial protest, “Should we take the subway or a squad car?”

“Car. Now…where are we going for lunch?”

Chapter 14

Jenkins knew the building in Brooklyn that they were headed to. It used to be the Long Island headquarters of the company he had worked for years ago. He didn't want to relay that to the men he was with just yet. It would be just another tidbit of information that tied him to the case and he really didn't want that, especially with people like Detective Vestapool around. Jenkins was sitting in the back seat with Tim Ford. Tommy Boyle was driving and Brad Tolliver was riding shotgun. Jenkins thoughts went back to a different time as he looked out at Brooklyn from the back seat of a squad car going over the Brooklyn bridge.

When they finally arrived at 101 Willoughby Street in Brooklyn it was 2:30PM. There was a squad car on each block surrounding the building. No one had seen anything unusual or any clues. As Jenkins got out of the car, he looked up at the art deco building which was built in the 1930's and recalled the times he had been here before on business. He had always admired this building's architecture. It had recently been converted to high priced condominiums which saddened him, but at least it had become a historical landmark.

The four men had been talking, mostly small talk, but now they were deciding what to do and what they should be looking for. Maybe this was a waste of time. Maybe it was a trap. It's not likely that the killer would try anything in broad daylight on the streets of Brooklyn, but you never know. They took a walk around the building and came back to the Willoughby side. Jenkins said he wanted to go back to the other side of the building just to check out something. It was almost 3PM.

At about 3:07 the others heard a woman screaming. They could not tell where it was coming from. Boyle realized it was probably *coming from above and he rushed into the* building. Ford was right behind him. Tolliver got on the radio to see if the other units had seen or heard anything. They contemplated taking the stairs, but the building was at least 25 floors. They anxiously waited for the elevator. When the doors opened one person came out. They grabbed her and asked her if she saw anything on the higher floors. She nervously said that she had not. They rushed past her. They decided to go to the highest floor and work their way down by stairs.

Vera Farnon knew her life was over when someone grabbed her from behind on her 23rd floor roof patio at 101 Willoughby Street in Brooklyn, New York. She tried to fight anyway. Then she screamed. The person who grabbed her picked her up off the floor, she screamed again, and then he threw her over the side. She screamed once more but only as long as it took to fall six stories. Then she was indeed dead. She landed on a 17th floor roof patio.

Tim Ford, Tommy Boyle and Brad Tolliver finally made their way down to the 23rd floor. A male resident told them he had heard a scream coming from a condo on that floor. They pulled out their guns and forcibly entered the condo. Jenkins showed up a few seconds later.

Tim Ford: “Where have you been?”

Mark Jenkins: “I was waiting for an elevator.”

Ford: “Did you hear the screaming?”

Jenkins: “Yes.”

They all went out to the rooftop patio and looked over the side. After a while they saw Vera Farnon’s body laying six floors below.

Tommy Boyle: “Do we know what floor that is?”

Jenkins: “According to the building chart it should be the 17th.”

Boyle: “Let’s go!”

They were able to gain access to the 17th floor patio through a maintenance hallway. Tommy Boyle checked to see if Farnon was alive. “She’s dead.”

Uniforms arrived shortly after. Vera Farnon's condo on the 23rd floor was searched and so was her body on the 17th floor. The leaf that was in her mouth along with the note found under her body were placed in separate plastic evidence bags.

It was after 5 before they wrapped up and headed back to Manhattan. It was after 6 before they got back to the precinct. The trip back was solemn. At the precinct Tolliver told the others to go home and get some good sleep. "Let's start a little earlier tomorrow."

"What time?"

"How's 8:30 sound?"

"8:30 is fine."

"See you then."

Chapter 15

The next day they all gathered in the conference room again. It was the same group as the day before minus Sherriff Harrington. He was on his way back to Sot Strom.

Mark Jenkins consultant, Lieutenant Tommy Boyle NYPD, Agent Don Holzer FBI, Agent Jeff Bullis FBI, Agent Carol Foster FBI, Captain Brad Tolliver NYPD, Detective Tim Ford NYPD, Detective Duncan Vestapool NYPD, and Detective Lucy York NYPD were sitting around the conference table in seemingly the same seats as the day before. Officer Reilly entered the room and brought a folder to Captain Brad Tolliver. When Reilly left the room, Tolliver began to speak. He talked about the events of the previous day. Then he pulled out the note that had been found under Vera Farnon's body. It was in a plastic evidence bag and it read "I am Vi".

Agent Carol Foster brought up a similar case that she had worked on in Seattle. Boyle brought up "The Son of Sam" David Berkowitz. Agent Holzer brought up Joel Rifkin. Jenkins brought up the Zodiac killer. There was a lot of discussion on each but no true direction to the conversation. Until Jenkins said, "It could be Virgo…. I am Virgo." There was silence as they all contemplated it.

Then Tolliver said, "So you think we have another Zodiac killer?"

“Well not exactly, but… yeah.”
They all seemed to think that was possible.

Tolliver looked up from the note and said, “Well we can’t let him get the whole word spelled out. That means at least three more bodies. Lieutenant you and Jenkins go to the Medical Examiner and see what you can find out about the murder weapon and those leaves.”

Agent Foster asked if she could tag along to the M.E. All agreed.

Agent Don Holzer said that he and Agent Bullis were going to travel around the tri-state area and talk to family and friends of the victims to see if there were any common threads. Holzer and Tolliver agreed that the group should reconvene the next morning.

Back in Sot Strom Sheriff Harrington was sitting at his desk at the Sot Strom cop shop sipping tea. Perhaps a bit of Jenkins had rubbed off on him. Out the window he could see part of the Sot Strom Museum and part of the Sot Strom fire department. Between those buildings and past them he could see Colby Hill one of the smaller mountains in the area. He contemplated summers end as he spotted some leaves that had begun to lose their dark green colors and morph into brighter yellows and reds. He wasn't a big fan of winter, but he didn't mind the fall at all.

Deputy MacDonald knocked on the door and the sheriff invited him in.

"Sheriff, I got the information from Albany on the station wagon driver. His name was Edward Claxton, and he had an incurable cancer and would probably have died in a few months if... you know... Mr. Jenkins hadn't shot and killed him."

The sheriff pulled his gaze off of Colby Hill and waited for his eyes to adjust.

"So maybe suicide by cop?"

MacDonald continued, "Also says he's from Syracuse."

"Does he have any family?"

"Doesn't look like anyone living."

"Well, I'll have to call the feds and let them know."

"Okay Sheriff I'll get the rest of the documents printed."

"Thanks Johnny."

Sheriff Harrington sat at his desk contemplating calling Agent Holzer but drifting back to Colby Hill. He reminded himself that he should make a point of spending more time in nature. He did live in a great area for it. As he sipped his tea he slowly drifted back to reality and picked up the phone.

Chapter 16

Tommy Boyle, Agent Foster and Mark Jenkins arrived at the morgue. There they learned, as they suspected, that Vera Farnon died from blunt force trauma, i.e., the impact from the fall. The leaf in her mouth was from a cottonwood tree.

Jenkins thought for a few seconds and then asked, “Eastern Cottonwood?”

“Yes” replied the M.E.

“Does that mean something to you?” Agent Foster asked Jenkins.

“I'm not sure yet.”

Then the M.E. said, “There's something else. Elaine Shoeman had water in her eye wound. John Beckford had water in one of his stab wounds too. We think maybe the weapon was an icicle. Probably not the standard icicle that might hang from a building, but something stronger and sharpened to a point. More like an ice shard. My guess would be it was carved out of a block of ice in a very cold setting.”

Agent Foster said, “Wow, that's crazy.”

“Not really.” Jenkins replied.

“It would be a good weapon as far as not being able to recover it.” Boyle added.

The three of them went back to the precinct to go over information. First thing they wanted to solve was the leaf correlation. If there was one.

Boyle opened the discussion. "So, Elaine Shoeman had a Sugar Maple in her mouth. Jane Tyson had a Northern Red Oak. Tamika Wilson had a White Oak. John Beckford had no leaf. And Vera Farnon had a Cottonwood Leaf in her mouth. I have an idea."

Agent Foster said, "Do tell."

"I think I know what you're doing." said Jenkins.

"Let's look on the internet." Was Boyle's reply. Boyle then opened and turned on the laptop and Jenkins and Foster looked over his shoulder. "Elaine Shoeman was from Vermont. The state tree of Vermont is.... Sugar Maple. Coincidence? .... I think not." Boyle continued to type. "Jane Tyson was from New Jersey. State tree of New Jersey is.... Northern Red Oak. Tamika Wilson was from Connecticut. State tree of Connecticut is.... White Oak. John Beckford was from New York, but he had no leaf. We still don't know where Vera Farnon was from but I'm betting it's either Kansas or Nebraska."

"Yep, I thought about this at the morgue." Said Jenkins.

Detectives Vestapool and Ford knocked once on the door and came in. Vestapool spoke, "We just got back from Brooklyn only thing we found out is Vera Farnon was from Hutchinson, Kansas."

They felt like they had confirmation on their leaf correlation theory. They let the two detectives in on that information. They also had the icicle theory which might prove to be helpful. They all knew they needed a lot more to go on, but at least they were starting to gather evidence that they might be able to use.

After the leaf findings Vestapool seemed to be warming up a bit to Jenkins but he still had his doubts. He didn't like civilians that he didn't know working on police matters, no matter how close Jenkins seemed to be to his boss. In reality, Vestapool really didn't like civilians.

They all talked more about the leaf correlation. Why would the killer want to put their home state tree leaves in the mouths of each of the victims?

Agent Holzer and agent Bullis Were in Port Chester NY stopping for dinner on their way back from Greenwich Connecticut which was just across the state border. In Greenwich they had visited with a victim's family. They had taken notes on all prevalent information about Tamika Wilson. While they were eating, they were talking a bit about her when Holzer got a call from a number he did not recognize. He let it go to voice mail.

A bottle of Chilean cabernet sauvignon lays carefully wrapped in cloth at the bottom of a tote bag. Next to it lay two wine glasses also carefully and individually wrapped in cloth. Lucy York carries the tote bag down a hall to a door numbered 701. She pauses and listens, then, ignoring the do not disturb sign, she knocks firmly but not too hard, four times. She hears no stirring on the other side of the door and no one answers. She waits contemplating and then knocks again. Detective Lucy York is not one to pout, but she couldn't help but feel disappointed. She walked away leaving only one slight trace that she had been there, a faint whiff of her perfume.

After dinner Holzer and Bullis were back in the car and Holzer listened to his voicemail. It was from Harrington. Holzer called him back.
“Hi Jim, it’s Don Holzer. I got your message to call you back.”
“Hello Don. I wanted to let you know that the name of the station wagon driver was… um…. Edward Claxton and that he had terminal cancer. Claxton was from Syracuse NY.”
“Okay, got it.”
“Also, there are unknown prints in the car.”
“I see.”
Harrington continued, “I suggest you deal directly with CSI in Albany.”
“Why is that?”
“I just think it would be better and easier for you.”
“Okay thanks Jim”
“You’re welcome. Good night”
“Good night”

When Holzer hung up from Harrington, Agent Bullis who had been looking through the paperwork and his laptop said, “Maybe it’s a cop hater.”
Holzer replied, “what makes you say that?”
“Tamika Wilson’s brother is a C.O.”
“Any other victims related to cops?”
“I don’t know yet, it’s just a theory. I’ll check it out in the morning. Let’s get back to the city.”

Lieutenant Tommy Boyle, Agent Carol Foster, Mark Jenkins, Detective Tim Ford and Detective Duncan Vestapool were sitting around a table in the precinct with a couple of pizza boxes from Lombardi's. Boyle continued the conversation, "So to summarize, here's what we know: Some victims had their home state leaves in their mouths. Icicles may have been used. Notes were left on some of the victims. The killer knows, or knows of Jenkins. There's a possible connection to some type of Zodiac killer maybe Virgo.... Um ... that's really it. .... So, what are the logical questions?

Jenkins said, "Is there a connection between the victims?"

Foster said, "What is the killer's motive?"

Vestapool said, "What is the connection with Jenkins and what did what happened in Sot Strom have to do with it? Perhaps this is an organization or group of killers?"

Foster agreed, "It's hard to believe that someone just happened to be wanting to shoot up the Sot Strom police department while a couple of FBI agents were there. Ya know, Jenkins might just be a target too."

Jenkins gave a solemn smirk and Boyle said, "Yes, I have thought of that."

Jenkins said, "Me too."

Foster asked, "Did any of the local murders happen the same night as the Sot Strom incident?"

Boyle answered, "We don't think so."

Foster continued, “So it’s possible that the killer traveled up to Sot Strom and back, but it’s really starting to look like the detective might be on to something as far as it being an organization or a group.”

After a few moments of silence Ford said, “Perhaps the most pressing question is how can we predict where, when and who the next victim will be?”

Boyle agreed, “Well these are all good questions and we should think about them, but it’s getting late and we should all get some sleep.”

Chapter 17

The unlikely investigative team was gathering at the precinct. Lucy York caught up with Jenkins in the hall, "I stopped by your room last night. I thought you might want to talk about old times."

"Really? What time did you stop by?"

"Early evening."

"Oh…we were here late, working on the case."

"I see. I was also thirsty and horny and thought maybe you were too."

"Ha… um … I'm sure I'll be here at least a few more nights."

"ah… then I have something to look forward to?"

"okay… and I do too."

They all sat around the conference table again: Mark Jenkins consultant, Lieutenant Tommy Boyle NYPD, Agent Don Holzer FBI, Agent Jeff Bullis FBI, Agent Carol Foster FBI, Captain Brad Tolliver NYPD, Detective Tim Ford NYPD, Detective Duncan Vestapool NYPD, and Detective Lucy York NYPD. Tolliver again started the conversation. They all shared the information they had learned the day before. Foster, Boyle and Jenkins talked about the leaves and the possible use of icicles. Holzer and Bullis talked about a possible cop, ex-cop, or cop hater connection and the fact that Ed Claxton, the Sot Strom shooter, was terminally ill. Then they said that they'd be heading to New Jersey to meet with victim Jane Tyson's family after the meeting. Foster also brought up the possibility of a group or organization.

Just as they are getting ready to disperse and take their investigation in several different directions, officer Reilly knocks on the door. Tolliver tells him to come in.

"Captain, there's another body in Queens."

"Fuck! Okay let's go.... Tommy, Mark, and Carol come with me to Queens. Don and Jeff, you're off to New Jersey, right? The rest of you stay here and relay info and hold the fort down."

Lucy York spoke, "Captain can I go to Queens also?"

Tolliver agreed and they all left the room.

In Queens, on a desolate warehouse street lies the body of Steven Cushman. The team arrives and notices similar wounds to the other victims. Boyle and York check the body while Jenkins and Foster looked around the neighborhood. Boyle checked the mouth of the victim and saw no leaf. York however, did find a note in his pocket. The note said "I am Vir"

Brad Tolliver talked to the warehouse workers who found the body. Foster joined him and they collected as much information as the workers had.

Tommy Boyle saw Jenkins turn the corner outside at the end of the building. Jenkins looked like he was talking to someone. By the time Boyle turned the corner Mark was talking to a homeless man who was sitting on a flattened cardboard box up against the wall of the warehouse near a loading dock. Jenkins found out the homeless man's name was Bob. Boyle noticed that sitting near the homeless man was what looked like a brand-new umbrella.

When Boyle got close, Jenkins said to Bob, "This is my friend Tommy. He and I are investigating what or whom may have killed the man that was found dead right around this corner."

Boyle said, "Sir, did you see or hear anything?"

Bob just shook his head no.

Boyle gave Bob his business card and told him to call if he remembers or hears about anything that could relate.

Jenkins took out a twenty and gave it to Bob and said, "I'm sure you can put this to good use."

Bob thanked him. Boyle remembered that Jenkins was always generous to the homeless. Jenkins said to Bob, "Stay out of the rain if you can."

As Boyle and Jenkins were walking away Jenkins said, "See you later, Bob." Boyle thought to himself that Jenkins said it like he really meant he would see Bob later and he wondered to himself why it sounded like that.

Agent Don Holzer was looking at house addresses as Agent Jeff Bullis drove. Bullis spoke, “That’s it 107 Woodward.”
They were in Rutherford, New Jersey and had just arrived at the Tyson residence. They were preparing to talk to the family of victim Jane Tyson. Neither Bullis, nor Holzer, liked this part of the job, but it needed to be done. They knew that any information they could get might help them narrow down who this killer was and stop *these murders. Even if they only saved one* life, it was all worth it. At least that’s how they knew they should have felt. Often it was more about the paycheck, the benefits and the pension. They solemnly approached the house, a house they knew would be yet another house of mourning. Bullis took a deep breath and pressed the doorbell.

Workers for the coroner were loading the body into the van in Queens, New York. Tolliver, Boyle, Jenkins, Foster and York were discussing the crime.
York spoke, “It fits the pattern but no leaf.”
Boyle said, “Well, we don’t know that for sure, it may have slipped down his throat. We’ll have to wait for the coroner’s report.”
Brad Tolliver was visibly upset. “I hate these cases. We have to wait for someone else to get murdered to get little tidbits of evidence

that will not likely save the next potential victim."

After the coroner left, they separated into two groups and walked the neighborhood. It was not likely they would find any new information, they knew that, but there was not much else to do. Being an industrial neighborhood and not residential there were likely no witnesses, except maybe for a homeless person here and there. The crime likely took place at night which also made witnesses scarce in this neighborhood. They talked to some workers at other warehouses to no avail.

An hour had passed since the coroner left when Tolliver decided they should head back to the precinct. They got into the two squad cars and drove back to Manhattan. There was plenty of paperwork to do and a lot of research as well.

Chapter 18

The next day at the morning meeting information was shared and questions were asked. Foster asked why Cushman and Beckford had no leaves. They were also the only male victims. Was there a correlation? Bullis and Holzer said that Jane Tyson's mother was a retired police officer in New Jersey. So, the cop connection theory was looking stronger. Bullis also said that the fingerprints on the station wagon in Sot Strom came back as being blocked in the system. Suggesting a high-level person or some insider hacking.

Brad Tolliver had laid out a map of the City on the conference room table. He was looking at the Queens warehouse neighborhood where the most recent body was found. He then said, "There's an ice cream and ice warehouse about two blocks from where the body was found yesterday. I would like Tommy, Tim, and Duncan to check it out."

Foster said that she and Bullis and Holzer would work the FBI database from the FBI offices in Manhattan and try to pull up more information. She now believed it was an inside job as in either a cop, ex-cop, an agent or an ex-agent.

Tolliver then asked Jenkins to go to the M.E. to see if there was a way to tell if the leaves were frozen and if not, where would the killer be getting these leaves. Lucy York asked if she could go with Jenkins. Brad agreed.

Then Brad said, “I’ll be in my office hoping I don’t get a call about another body and trying to figure out what I’m going to tell the commissioner.”

Needless to say, it was cold in the ice cream warehouse. Boyle, Ford and Vestapool were trying to find the manager. An employee *dressed in winter clothes complete with gloves* and hat told them where the manager’s office was. After talking to the manager for a few minutes they asked if they could look around the warehouse. After about a half hour of looking around they went outside to warm up. They all got coffee from the coffee cart. After the break they went back in. In a corner on the far side about as far away from the main door as one could get, they found little shards of ice. Nothing of any size that could be used to stab someone the way their victims were stabbed, but they could tell that someone had done some ice carving back there. They questioned the employees, but no significant information was acquired.

Boyle got back in the car and spoke. “Damn I don’t think I’ve ever been this cold in September.”

Ford said, “Yeah that sucked.”

Boyle: “I wonder why Brad didn’t send Jenkins here. He loves the cold.”

Vestapool: “Really, he likes the cold? That’s interesting.”
Boyle: “How so?”
Vestapool: “Just is.”

Boyle decided to drive the two blocks over to where Steven Cushman’s body had been found. He looked around then took a walk around the corner to see if the homeless guy Bob was still there. He wasn’t. There was no trace of him, no cardboard’ no belongings.
Ford asked, “What are you doing?”
Boyle: “Just looking for something.”

At the New York City FBI offices Foster Bullis and Holzer were discussing their findings. Victim Elaine Shoeman’s father is a retired cop in Burlington, Vermont. Victim John Beckford’s uncle is a cop in Portland, Maine. Victim Vera Farnon’s father is a retired Kansas state trooper. Victim Steve Cushman’s two sisters are cops in San Francisco.
Foster: “I guess we can come to two conclusions. One - the victims have something in common. And two - there is a cop connection.”
Holzer: “No doubt. Not sure how this will help us find our suspect or suspects.”
Bullis: “I guess we’ll see what the others can come up with at the morning meeting tomorrow”

Mark Jenkins and Lucy York, no doubt, had some sexual tension building as they arrived at the coroner's office. Jenkins held the door open for York and they entered. The coroner told them that the leaves were likely frozen in ice. One of the crime scene investigators on hand said, "Picture leaves in a block of ice." Then they were likely cut out and carefully handled until being placed in the mouths of the victims.

Jenkins and York were surprised how late it was by the time they got out of the M.E.s office. It was almost lunch time and they decided to go to a bar for lunch. Jenkins always liked to sit at the bar. He rarely sat at a table. This time was no different. He and York sat at the bar and had lunch and a couple of beers. They shared small talk with the bartender. They even told him they were investigating a series of murders in the New York City vicinity. York was surprised how open Jenkins seemed. She remembered him being more guarded. However, he didn't reveal any inside information about the case to the bartender.

After lunch they headed back to the precinct to check in and see if there were any new developments. They had barely gotten in the precinct door when Jenkins cell started ringing. Brad's name came on the screen.

"Hey Brad."

"Where are you?"

"Just got back to the precinct."

"Head to the ferry."
"Staten Island?"
"Yeah."
"Another body?"
"Yeah. Is York with you?
"Yes."
"Bring her too."

On a blood-stained grassy area between the 911 memorial in Staten Island and the Staten Island Yankees stadium lay the body of Ronald Sexton. Jenkins and York had unknowingly been on the same ferry as Boyle and Ford. The rest of their investigative team stayed back in Manhattan busying themselves with various tasks. When Mark Jenkins, Lucy York, Tommy Boyle and Tim Ford arrived at the scene, Boyle asked to speak to whomever was in charge. After talking to other police officers and witnesses, they had discovered that Sexton was heard bragging the night before at a bar called Ruddy and Dean about how he was an ex-marine and he was a mixed martial arts expert.

Boyle said, "Apparently, he was no match for our killer with an icicle."

An officer brought a plastic bag to Boyle with a note. It said, "I am Virg."

Borrowing some latex gloves Boyle and Ford went to Sexton's body. While Boyle grabbed the head, he was suddenly holding a patch of hair. Apparently, Sexton wore a hair piece.

Boyle then grabbed both sides of the head and Ford opened the mouth. There was no leaf. After some more discussion with the local precinct cops, Boyle asked that any other evidence they find be sent over to his office.

Boyle turned to Jenkins, “I guess there’s no doubt now. It’s got to be Virgo.”

Jenkins replied, “Yes… unless it’s Virgil the frog boy.”

Boyle smirked then chuckled, “Remember *that shit?*”

Chapter 19

On the ferry back to Manhattan Mark Jenkins and Lucy York found a spot upstairs on the outside deck. The sun was setting behind the Statue of Liberty. Jenkins spoke, “Kind of romantic, isn’t it?”

York replied, “Yes.”

Just then Boyle and Ford joined them. They discussed the case for a few minutes. Then the conversation changed to what a great city New York is and how the Staten Island Ferry is a great way to see it. Jenkins suggested that when they get off the boat, they all go have a beer at Fraunces Tavern. All agreed.

After two beers Boyle said he had to go. Ford went with him. When they got outside Ford said to Boyle, “You think they’re fucking?”

Boyle replied, “I don’t know. It’s none of my business. Not very professional, but still, none of my business.

Jenkins and York had one more beer and talked about old times. They also planned to have a “date” the next evening if circumstances allowed it. The conversation then switched to the case. York said she had a theory that it was a five-person murderous gang. One person for each letter of the word Virgo. Jenkins tells her that’s a good theory and that she should bring it up at the morning meeting.

York looked at Jenkins with a playful smirk, "Are you going to tell me what that frog boy thing was about?"

Jenkins: "Oh yeah. When we were growing up there was this train trestle the next town over. Going back as far as we can remember it always said 'Virgil is the frog boy' in graffiti. They would paint over it and it would be back up there the next day. No one knows who painted it, but they would have to put themselves in a difficult position to do it, by either standing on the tracks and leaning over the side to write upside down, or by hanging on the side of the trestle over the roadway. Then years later it was still there, and they painted over it again and the next day it said, 'Virgil is still the frog boy' then years after that they painted over it again and the next day it said, 'Virgil will always be the frog boy.'"

York listened, smiled and then laughed when Jenkins was finished explaining the frog boy story.

After a few moments of silence, she turned to him and gazed at him admiringly. "You know, I could have married you."

Jenkins looked back at her contemplating the scenario and studying her admiring gaze. After a while he said, "Being married to me would have killed you."

Chapter 20

The gathering for the morning meeting was becoming routine. Several team members would get coffee, some would get donuts, some would get a buttered roll, others water and some preferred nothing. Jenkins always had a bottle of water. He looked around the room as they waited for Brad to come in and start the meeting. Everyone seemed anxious and ready to go.

Brad Tolliver walked in and said, "Okay let's go around the table and see what everyone has."

Tommy Boyle, Tim Ford and Duncan Vestapool talked about the ice shards at the ice and ice cream warehouse. Agents Don Holzer, Carol Foster and Jeff Bullis shared their cop connection information. York and Jenkins talked about the leaves and how they had been frozen in ice. Then they all talked about the latest Staten Island victim Ronald Sexton.

Boyle said, "Ya know other than the bodies that were found in Jersey and Connecticut there were bodies found in every borough but the Bronx. Perhaps we should put them on alert?" Brad thought that was a good idea. Then York brought up the five-person theory. She said that perhaps there was one person for each letter in Virgo. The team seemed to think that was an interesting idea. Then Brad said, "If this is a group or gang this is going to be more difficult than I imagined, but can we assume that this group, if there is one, has a ringleader. If so, what can we profile from the information we have now?"

This particular morning meeting was longer than previous ones. The profile they painted was a highly intelligent, highly motivated male cop hater and possible misogynist who was probably beyond reason and would not likely stop killing until he was dead or in prison.

After much discussion Brad started to bring the meeting to a close and asked that the team, "stay close and not go out into the field today. Work together and brainstorm. I have a meeting with the commissioner."

As the meeting broke up officer Reilly passed Ford and Vestapool in the hall and said, "Did you hear about Buddy McMillan?"

"No. What happened?"

"He collapsed in the street about an hour ago. He's in the hospital."

"Is he okay?"

"Don't know yet. I'm going to try to get over there at lunch time to see him."

Buddy McMillan was an old-fashioned beat cop. He liked to walk his precinct and talk to people and make sure they all knew he was in charge. He lived in Nassau County out on Long Island and took the Long Island Railroad to work every day. It was a good thing he preferred to walk because he had a tendency to drink. Also, his captain, Brad Tolliver, did not want him driving after he used his badge to get out of a DWI charge out on Long Island a few years before. His fellow officers liked him for his humor, brash pro cop attitude and his propensity to tell stories of the old days. Such stories usually involved, "knocking some punks heads together."

But now Buddy McMillan laid in a hospital bed. He had been brought in by ambulance and was feeling extremely sick. The doctors had yet to tell him what was wrong with him. He remembered walking down the street and passing a gentleman. The gentleman then apologized to McMillan for accidentally hitting McMillan's leg with his umbrella. Buddy was lying there thinking it was odd that someone was carrying an umbrella on such a sunny day.

Chapter 21

Brad Tolliver gathered the team for a rare late afternoon meeting. He told them that he had just come from the meeting with the commissioner. Although he did not appear to be shaken, Jenkins knew that he was, especially when he said he could use a big, tall whiskey. He then addressed the group while looking at York and stated firmly, “This is not a gang! It is one person!”

The investigative team stayed late that night discussing their profile of the killer which was a highly intelligent, highly motivated male, cop hater and possible misogynist who was probably beyond reason and would not likely stop killing until he was dead.

Agent Carol Foster asked, “If this is a cop hater, why is he not targeting cops instead of their family members?

Tommy Boyle said, “Maybe he wants to hurt cops. Perhaps he feels that killing a cop is not as satisfying as taking away someone they love.”

At that point in time almost everyone in the room got on their phones and made calls to loved ones.

Once the phone calls were over Boyle suggested going to the media to which Brad replied that he would have to check with the commissioner’s office first.

They broke into groups and started looking over the surveillance videos to see if they could find something the tech analyst had missed.

After a few hours they found two videos and it looked like the same man was in both. One was near 101 Willoughby in Brooklyn not long after Vera Farnon was murdered there. The other was in Tribeca close to the time that John Beckford was murdered. Neither image was clear, but it did look like the same man in similar clothing on each video. It would be a hell of a coincidence. Jenkins was the only one who expressed doubts about it being the same man.

Tolliver came around to the team and told them it was late and to go home and get some rest.

By the next morning they were cleared to use the media. The commissioner wanted to make the statement at the press conference himself that evening. The team spent most of the morning getting their reports together so the commissioner's speech writer could put together a viable announcement. The hope was to get the public's help in solving the case without causing widespread panic.

In the afternoon they tried another brainstorming session, but they came up with nothing new. Tolliver suggested that they all take off early and get some rest after all they had been working long hours the last few days. He also told them to be sure to watch the press conference that evening.

Jenkins decided to go back to his room at the Ritz and take a nap before going out to get dinner. On his way out the door of the precinct Lucy York said to him, "Maybe get together later?"

"Sounds good. I'll call you."

"So, you say." She smirked.

The rest of the team members used the afternoon to make sure their family members were okay and imploring them not to follow their usual routines for the next few days.

Boyle decided to send his wife and kids out to the Hamptons. It was after Labor Day and lodging out there was slightly more affordable than before Labor Day. He told his wife to stay out there and don't tell anyone where she was until he told her otherwise.

Other team members were taking similar precautions with their family members. There would probably be a lot more of it going on after the press conference.

A few hours after leaving the precinct Jenkins was in a bar sipping a tasty craft beer and watching the screen for the press *conference that was about to take place*. He turned to his left and said, "You ready for this?"
Lucy York said, "Yeah. Why do you ask?
Jenkins replied, "Well it should be interesting. The commissioner is about to speak on the very case we are working on."
York said, "Does this excite you?"
Jenkins: "A little."
York: "I could probably think of something that might excite you more."
Jenkins just smiled.

The commissioner's announcement began. He started out by saying not to panic then went on to talk about a probable serial killer who seemed to be targeting families of police officers. He went on to say that they believe the individual calls himself "Virgo." He did not go into the details of any of the murders or where they were. Then at the end of his announcement he made a plea to Virgo looking straight at the camera. He asked Virgo to be merciful and to remember that these were human beings. He went on to say that Virgo must have had people in his life that he cared for and who cared for him.

Jenkins cringed at this part of the announcement and said, "Whoa, that is not a good idea."

The commissioner went on to say that if Virgo had a bad experience with a police officer to remember that most police officers are good people and are here to serve and protect the public.

Jenkins cringed again, "Ugh, strike two."

The commissioner went on to urge Virgo to turn himself in and promised he would be treated fairly.

Jenkins said, "Strike three."

York said, "Didn't he read the profile we sent him? Fucking politician!"

Jenkins: "Oh well. Speaking of fucking."

York: "Let's get out of here."

Tommy Boyle got on the phone. "Brad, what the fuck was that? He looked more like a politician than someone trying to get the public's help to track down a serial killer."

Brad Tolliver: "Holy shit, I know. There's nothing we can do about it."

Boyle: "This isn't good. We don't know how 'Virgo' will react."

Tolliver: "I agree. But I guess we'll find out. See you tomorrow."

Boyle: "Goodnight."

Room 107 at the Woodcalling Hotel has very thin walls, but Lucy York and Mark Jenkins didn't care. It had been a while since either had gotten laid. They both laid there entangled in each other and slightly out of breath.
Jenkins: "That was great."
York: "Agreed"
After about ten minutes...
York: "What do you think the fallout will be of the commissioner's gig?"
Jenkins: "I don't think it will be good. On the other hand, it may not rattle Virgo at all. Guess we'll have to wait and see."

Chapter 22

The next day the team gathered and discussed the commissioners stunt the night before. The phones at the precinct were constantly ringing with people wanting to report that they knew Virgo or knew a Virgo and some even said that they were Virgo. The ones that claimed to be Virgo were asked specifics about the case and were all dismissed as "pranks" or "crazies." Brad told the team there's not much to do except brainstorm and wait. After a half hour of brainstorming the room fell silent. Duncan Vestapoole pulled out a deck of cards and started playing cards with Tim Ford. The others were in and out of the conference room getting coffee and walking around. Jenkins went out to get some air. Time seemed to be really dragging on this day for most of the team. Agent Holzer asked if everyone had taken precautions for their families. All had. Agent Bullis asked officer Reilly how Buddy McMillian was doing. Reilly told him that McMillian was not getting better and that the doctors didn't know what was wrong with him yet.

They all went out for lunch except Ford and Vestapoole they ordered in. Brad told the ones who did go out to keep their phones handy.

After lunch there was still no news. They gathered in the conference room again for another brainstorming session. First, they watched the commissioner's speech at the press conference again and shook their heads in disbelief. Then they discussed the profile and talked about the videos. They all got up to look at the videos again. The tech had gotten the video picture to be much clearer, but one could not see the man's face in either video. There wasn't much else to go on, so they waited some more.

Finally, in the late afternoon Brad addressed the team and said, "Maybe the commissioner's stunt worked. How about we all take the day off tomorrow, get some rest and get a fresh start on Monday."

Everyone seemed to agree.

Officer Declan Reilly had been on the force for eight years. He liked his job. One of his fondest mentors was Buddy McMillian. At the end of his shift, he went to the hospital to check on Buddy. When he got to the floor of the hospital that McMillian's room was on, he could hear someone yelling for a crash cart. He got to McMillian's room in time to watch the medical team try to revive him. Almost five grueling minutes later the doctor called the time of death.

Reilly stayed with his mentor's body for a while with a lump in his throat and wet eyes. Then he called Duncan Vestapoole to tell him. Vestapoole told Reilly he'd be down in a few minutes.

Vestapoole arrived with Tim Ford and the three men mourned the loss of their comrade. Vestapoole was over by the EKG machine and the nurse begged his pardon as she went around him to get the EKG machine and wheel it out of the room. As she was wheeling it out Vestapoole almost yelling said, "Hold it!" to the nurse. She stopped in her tracks. Vestapoole then went over to the EKG machine and looked at the back. He thought he had seen something on the back of the machine.

Just then Tommy Boyle arrived with Mark Jenkins. Vestapoole reached out to the back of the machine and pulled off a post-it note. The note said, “I am Virgo!”

Jenkins told the nurse to go get the doctor in charge. When the doctor arrived, Boyle told the doctor to “check this body for any puncture or needle marks that you or your staff did not administer.”

Boyle, Jenkins, Vestapoole, Ford and Reilly waited outside the room for the doctor and his staff to check McMillian’s body. After a few minutes, the doctor called them in and showed them a puncture wound behind McMillian’s left knee. Boyle and Jenkins looked at each other and said at the same time, “Bulgarian umbrella.”

Reilly then said, “What the fuck is a Bulgarian umbrella?”

Boyle ignored Reilly and said to the doctor, “Have him tested for Ricin.”

After paying their last respects to Buddy, Boyle, Jenkins, Vestapoole, Ford and Reilly left the hospital. On their way out the others paid their condolences to Reilly.

Jenkins and Boyle split off from the others and Boyle said to Jenkins, “So much for a day off.”

Jenkins replied, “See you tomorrow.”

The next morning things at the precinct were very solemn as they continued to mourn one of their own. The investigative team gathered again in the conference room. This time Brad Tolliver let Tommy Boyle do the talking. “Jenkins and I believe that Buddy McMillian was attacked on the street and that a Bulgarian umbrella was used. A Bulgarian umbrella is an umbrella with a hidden pneumatic mechanism which injects a small poisonous pellet containing Ricin. It has a hollowed stalk into which the pellet sits. We also believe that we’ve seen the actual umbrella that was used and that we know who used it.”

The mood in the room changed to one of hope as everyone paid close attention.

Then Jenkins chimed in, “We met a ‘homeless’ man who called himself Bob at the warehouse in Long Island City where Steven Cushman’s body was found. Although he was dressed in ragged clothing and was otherwise pretty dirty, he did have what looked like a brand-new umbrella.”

Then Boyle added, “We had no idea at the time and did not make any kind of connection, but now it's obvious that the umbrella could have been a Bulgarian umbrella. The tox report hasn't come from the hospital yet but I'm confident they will find Ricin."

Jenkins then said, "And most importantly Tommy and I both saw 'Bob' and can ID him."

Vestapoole said, "Reilly was saying that Buddy was wondering why the guy that bumped into him was carrying an umbrella on such a sunny day."

Tolliver looked at Jenkins and Boyle, "Okay why don't you guys go down to composite and see if they can put a face together for you. Then we'll get it out to the media and see if we get any hits."

Everything had changed. Now Virgo was a cop killer or cops killer. Police officers all over the city were angry and on edge. Which was in and of itself not safe for the public. It's not safe to have a city-wide police force with itchy trigger fingers. Specially in a city as large as New York. But they also had new hope and there was finally a general feeling among the team that they could stop Virgo.

Mark Jenkins and Tommy Boyle had been working for over an hour with the composite artist and a sketch artist to put together an image of the homeless man they had met at the warehouse. A likeness of Bob was starting to form on the screen. Then the phone rang on the desk. It was Brad. He wanted them both in his office right away. The composite was almost finished, but it would have to wait. Obviously, Brad had something important to tell them or perhaps to scold them about something.

When they got to Brad's office there was another man already there with Brad. Neither Jenkins nor Boyle knew who he was. Brad introduced him, "This is Jeff Johnson, he is an editor with the Daily News. He received a classified ad from Virgo and instead of printing it he came here to tell us about it."

Boyle: "What did the ad say?"

Johnson: "I brought a copy."

Brad Tolliver handed Tommy Boyle the printout. Boyle read it out loud: "Commissioner, cops are control freaks. Cops are wife beaters. Cops prey on the weak. Cops hide behind the badge and gun. Cops drink and drive. They break the law all the time. They do not serve and protect; they exploit and victimize. We should all hate cops. VIRGO"

They all thanked Johnson for bringing it down. Brad told him they would have a computer tech come to his office to see if they could trace where the ad came from. When Johnson left Boyle said, “Well, I guess we know that he saw the commissioner’s television appearance.”

Jenkins then said, “Yes, and we also know that this is not over.”

Chapter 23

The next day, after the morning meeting, the team's mood was more hopeful and determined than it had been. Tommy Boyle grabbed Mark Jenkins in the hall, "The computer composite sketch is finished, but I want to make sure you agree with it before we send it out to the media."

Jenkins said, "Okay, let's go down there and look at it."

As the elevator doors closed Boyle saw Lucy York give Jenkins a smile. As the elevator started to descend Boyle asked, "You hitting that?"

Jenkins smirked but didn't answer. So, Boyle continued, "Seriously? You're not gonna answer?"

Then Jenkins replied, "A gentleman never tells, and a gentleman never asks."

Boyle countered, "Yeah, but I'm asking you."

They both laughed and Boyle said, "She is pretty hot."

Down in composite they both looked at the face on the computer. Jenkins suggested some minor changes and then both he and Boyle concluded that it was ready. The posters were soon printed. Boyle and Jenkins took one up to show Captain Brad Tolliver. Brad said, “Good work. We’ll get them out to the media and out on the streets this afternoon. Hopefully, we’ll have a hit so we can zero in on this asshole.”

Jenkins feeling sheepish said, “Hey Brad I’m sorry I didn’t recognize that this guy could have been a suspect when I met him.”

Boyle jumped in, “I should have suspected him too.”

Tolliver assured them that it was not their fault. Virgo was obviously a slick character or a slick gang. Brad then assured them that with the composite going out they should have a sighting within a day or two.

Boyle asked, “What should we do in the meantime?”

Tolliver answered, “There’s not much to do. If you want to brainstorm or do more research that’s okay with me.”

Jenkins asked, “How does the commissioner feel about the composite going out?”

Tolliver said, “I’m not telling him.” and then almost a whisper, “I need a big, tall whiskey.”

Jenkins had had enough brainstorming for a while. He decided to do some research on the desktop computer in one of the cubicles. He told Boyle he'd catch up with him later.

After about an hour being at the computer Jenkins read on the screen Ricin is classified as a type 2 ribosome-inactivating protein (RIP). Then he said out loud "Two RIP. Rest in peace Bob." He didn't realize that Boyle was nearby and heard him. "What's that?"

"Jeez you startled me."

"Ha. Calm down. Brad wants to know if you want to go to lunch. Just the three of us.

"Yeah, sounds good."

For a while, while the three men were at lunch, it seemed like old times. Boyle and Jenkins talked about Virgil the frog boy and the three of them reminisced about parties and fishing trips of the old days. But then about halfway through lunch the conversation came back to Virgo and the case that had been confounding them for weeks now. That's when Brad ordered a big, tall whiskey. Of course, then they discussed what the commissioner's reaction might be to the composite going out. Then Boyle said, "You know there's a real good chance that he'll see it."

Tolliver asked, "Who the commissioner?"

"No. Virgo or Bob whatever his name is."

Jenkins chimed in, "He probably will. And we have no way of knowing how he will react."

Boyle said, "He could pack up and leave."

Jenkins, "I don't think so. He's too much of a narcissist."

Tolliver, "Well let's just hope one of our good citizens spot him before he does see it."

Lunch was tasty and the drinks were too, but it was time to get back to the precinct. The composite would be out to the public soon and the commissioner would know about it shortly after.

Back at the precinct all was quiet for the first ten minutes after lunch, but then the phones started ringing. Some of the mid-day news programs were broadcasting the story and the composite likeness of a person that Jenkins and Boyle knew only as "Bob."

Flyers were also being handed out in the streets by patrolmen. It wouldn't be long before word got to the commissioner.

Boyle, Jenkins, Detective Lucy York, Detective Tim Ford, Detective Duncan Vestapool, Agent Don Holzer Agent Jeff Bullis and Agent Carol Foster, were all asked to man the phones by Brad Tolliver. Then Tolliver got the expected call and as predicted the commissioner was not happy at all. Tolliver hung up the phone and announced, “He’s coming down here.” None of them were happy about that. Tolliver employed his stash of mouthwash and breath mints in preparation for the visit.

Tommy Boyle got a call that sounded like it could be something. He wrote a note and held it up for Mark Jenkins while he talked to the caller. The caller talked about a man fitting the description of the composite seen on the news. The caller said that the man was carrying a cooler and an umbrella in Long Island City. When he hung up, he and Jenkins went to see Brad. Brad told them to check the surveillance cameras in the area and see if they pick up anything. One of the cameras picked up a person carrying a cooler and an umbrella and going into what appeared to be an abandoned warehouse.

While they were on the computer checking the surveillance cameras, the commissioner showed up. Brad was getting an earful about how he needed to keep the commissioner informed about every detail of the Virgo case. Brad asked for forgiveness and promised to keep the commissioner informed.

As soon as the commissioner was gone. Jenkins and Boyle went into Tolliver's office, "We think we have something."

They proceeded to tell Brad that the sighting near the warehouse seemed to be their man, and that the suspect had disappeared into a warehouse. Then the phone rang. The computer tech had traced the IP address of where the classified ad had come from. It was the same warehouse.

Tolliver soon ordered a stake out of the warehouse in question. It was only a few blocks from where Steven Cushman's body was found and only a few blocks from the ice cream/ice warehouse. The team collectively thought that this was Virgo's headquarters.

During the first night of surveillance no one goes in or out of the warehouse, however several shadows and at least one silhouette is seen moving around on the upper floors. The two doors were on opposite sides of the building on the east and west respectively. There was also a garage door on the north side. It's an eight-story building with a fire escape coming down from the roof. Tolliver believed that waiting it out was the best way. If Virgo was in there, he was not out on the street killing people.

Chapter 24

In the morning Brad Tolliver got the surveillance report. "We have to keep surveillance up 24 hours a day. They have to come out sometime."

Tommy Boyle said, "Do you have to let the commissioner know?"

"Yes, I do."

Brad then went to his office to call and invite the commissioner to the precinct for a briefing on the Virgo case.

When the commissioner got the report, he ordered a tactical team full strike on the warehouse. He did not want to take any chances.

Brad Tolliver: "I do not think this is a good idea."

Commissioner: "Why?"

Tolliver: "I have a real bad feeling about this."

Commissioner: "What? A Fucking feeling?"

Tolliver: "This guy or gang is smart. Don't you think he or they might be ready for or even wanting an all-out assault? Can we at least see what the team thinks?"

Commissioner: "Sure. I'll humor you."

The two men left Brad's office and walked into the conference room where the team was gathered. Tolliver opened the conversation by saying that the Commissioner thought that a tactical team full strike on the warehouse was a good idea. Tommy Boyle, Mark Jenkins, Lucy York, Agent Jeff Bullis and Agent Carol Foster respectfully disagreed with the Commissioner. Agent Don Holzer said he wasn't sure.

Detectives Tim Ford and Duncan Vestapoole were all for it. They wanted to "go in and get the bastard." And they may have been sucking up to the commissioner, Tolliver thought.

The Commissioner said he would call FBI headquarters and let them know and to ask for assistance. Then he asked Tolliver to get it done as soon as possible. The team convinced the Commissioner that they would need some time to plan it and get it done. They all agreed that the next evening after rush hour would probably be best. In the meantime, the warehouse would be under surveillance. Though slightly skeptical that it was a delay tactic, the commissioner agreed to wait until the next evening.

After the meeting, the precinct was all of a buzz with talk of the tactical team full strike on the warehouse. Some were wondering who was going to be on the tactical team. The local precinct in Queens would have to get a shot at it to some capacity. But Brad was quite sure it would be led by his crew and the FBI.

There was a knock at Brad Tolliver's door.

Tolliver: "come in."

Officer Declan Reilly: "Captain, I was wondering if it would be okay for me to be on the tactical team tomorrow."

Tolliver just looked at him for a while then said, "Are you sure? This will be no picnic."

Reilly: "Yes sir. For Buddy's sake."

Tolliver reluctantly agreed, "Okay. Ford and Vestapoole will be point for our crew. Follow their orders."

Reilly: "Yes sir. Thank you, sir."

Boyle was talking to Jenkins in the break room, “I don’t think this is a good idea.”

Jenkins: “I don’t either.”

Boyle: “The commissioner is not going to change his mind.”

Jenkins: “I know. On the bright side, hopefully it will be over tomorrow.”

Boyle: “Yeah, hopefully, but at what cost?”

Captain Brad Tolliver gathered the team one more time in the conference room. He told them that if it was his call, he would not be doing the planned tactical team full strike. “We have no idea what is in that building and what is waiting for us, but this is what the commissioner wants. I’m not going to question authority on this one. I’m already in hot water. So, let’s go home and get a lot of sleep if we can. We can all start late tomorrow. It’s going to be a late night anyway.”

As they were all saying goodnight, Brad took Tommy Boyle aside and told him that he would be sending him an email letting him know that he was against this tactical team full strike, just so it would be on record before the incident. He’d be sending a similar email to the commissioner but worded more respectfully. It was a way of covering his ass so the mayor and everyone else would know this was not his call. If the full strike was successful, it would be no big deal, but if it wasn't, at least he had something predated in writing saying that he was against it.

That night the surveillance crew had a few men on the roofs of some buildings near the warehouse in question. They could see what looked like activity on the second, third and fourth floors. They could not see all the way in because the windows were not clear, but they could see shadows moving around periodically. This suggested there were more than one person. They set up electronic parabolic listening devices, but the building seemed to be surrounded by white noise as if blocked by electronic disrupters.

This was not good news to Brad. The tactical team would be going in nearly blind. He had little faith that he would sleep that night.

Chapter 25

Mark Jenkins woke up in Lucy York's apartment with her lying beside him. He had slept very well and was feeling horny. York had slept well too and was very receptive to his advance. They both knew that they didn't have to be in the precinct until late morning, so they proceeded to get it on.

A half hour later they were lying next to each other a little out of breath. Each had gotten up to use the restroom in turn. Then Jenkins got up and told York to stay where she was. He was going to make them tea.

After a while he returned with two steaming cups. The way Lucy looked at him with her big blue eyes he knew she adored him. He cared for her too. That's why he had to do what he had to do.

Once the tea was gone, they laid there talking and joking and laughing. Jenkins got up again and looked at her with a playful look. He told her to use the restroom which she did. When she came back, he grabbed her cell phone off the nightstand and brought it across the room and laid it on the dresser. He put his own cell phone next to it. Then he opened a drawer and got out a couple of sets of furry hand cuffs and ankle restraints. Lucy coyly smiled in anticipation as she let herself be cuffed to the bed. She was laying there naked with both wrists and both ankles secured to the bed. Jenkins touched her all over her body first with a feather then very lightly with his hands. After an hour she was crazy with lust and begged him to fuck her brains out. He obliged.

He left her secured to the bed and cleaned her up the best he could. Then he put the covers over her and went to take a shower. She shouted out to him how great the sex was and asked him to uncuff her from the bed. He said he had to take a shower and get ready to go to the precinct. She said that she had to also.

In the shower Jenkins felt both euphoric from the great sex and anxious about the day that lay ahead. While he was getting dressed Lucy York kept asking to be uncuffed, but Jenkins ignored her. Once he was ready, he went over to her and said, “I’m sorry about this, but it’s for your own good.” She protested emphatically. Jenkins told her he would be back that night. She was pretty pissed off, but she didn’t want to scream or alert her neighbors. After all, she was naked and if someone had to break the door down because of her sexual escapades she might lose her apartment.

Meanwhile Jenkins left the apartment, closed the door, locked it and went out into the day.

Mark Jenkins didn't arrive at the precinct until after 1PM. Brad Tolliver asked where he had been. He said he had been taking care of some personal things. Tolliver then asked if Jenkins had seen Lucy York to which Jenkins said that he had not. Tommy Boyle gave Jenkins a little ribbing saying that maybe he wore her out and she needed to rest. Brad seemed a little worried about York but she had done this once before so he figured maybe she was sick or that she and Jenkins had a fight and he would hear from her later. Brad had bigger things on his plate anyway.

At 2PM the heads of the tactical teams went over their plans. Tolliver, Boyle, Jenkins, Detective Tim Ford, Detective Duncan Vestapoole, Agent Don Holzer Agent Jeff Bullis and Agent Carol Foster were all there as well as some new faces none of them had ever seen. Vestapoole and Ford were to lead one team, Holzer and Bullis were to lead another and York and one of the Queens precinct detectives were going to lead the third. Since York had not been heard from, they were rethinking the third team's leaders. Carol Foster volunteered, but Tolliver asked her to stay in the van as the communication liaison for the feds. A second detective from the Queens precinct was selected instead. Boyle and Jenkins would be the other communication liaisons. Brad would be in the main van a block away and the other two vans would be about a half block away. Once the plan was laid out and everyone understood their part, the meeting broke up. Now there was nothing left to do but wait.

At 6PM they would start gathering gear and loading up the vehicles. Then they could head out about 6:30 or 7. Although there would still be a lot of traffic from rush hour, it was better than heading out at 5. It would start getting dark while they were in route and the cover of darkness could only help them.

Brad Tolliver sat nervously in his office awaiting the witching hour. Tommy Boyle and Mark Jenkins went in to talk to him.

Boyle: "What are you thinking about?"

Tolliver: "Wondering if there is a way to avoid this tactical assault."

Jenkins: "Did you try to reason with the commissioner again?"

Tolliver: "No"

Boyle: "Why not give him a call?"

Jenkins: "Or call the mayor."

Tolliver: "I'm not going to call the mayor. But maybe I can try the commissioner one more time."

Brad made the phone call and it was of no use. The commissioner wanted a tactical team full strike and he wanted it that evening. The commissioner had also scheduled a press conference for the next morning, most likely to pat himself on the back.

When Brad hung up the phone, he let out a long sigh. It was on. The three men sat in silence for a while it was nearing 4:30. Mark stood up and left Brad's office. He returned about 6 minutes later with three cold beers. The three friends sat and had a beer together pondering the evening ahead.

Tolliver broke the silence: "I'm not going to lie; I have a real bad feeling about this."

Boyle: "You don't have to go through with it!"

Tolliver: "Then I'd be insubordinate and possibly lose my pension."

Jenkins: "You can still call it off."

Tolliver: "The commissioner would then go around me and still make it happen."

Jenkins: "So you're just a soldier taking orders?"

Tolliver was visibly upset: "What the hell is that supposed to mean?"

Jenkins: "Nothing. I'm just saying you can take yourself out of it."

Boyle: "I'm sure Mark didn't mean anything offensive. And you're right the commissioner will get this done with or without you."

Tolliver: "I can't afford to risk my pension."

Jenkins: "That's completely understandable. I'm sorry if I offended you."

Tolliver was more somber: "This whole Virgo thing has me on edge."

Boyle: "Yes. We are all on edge. Let's order some pizza from Lombardi's and have a little pizza party before we get ready to go."

Tolliver: "Sounds good to me."

Jenkins: "Yeah, I love Lombardi's."

The squad cars and vans were driving with lights out as they pulled into place near the warehouse. The teams quietly got ready and moved into position waiting for the word from Tolliver. A team waited at each door on the east and west side of the building. Another team was at the loading door on the north side. If one team could not get through their assigned door a team that did get in would come around and open the other door or doors as the case would be. The surveillance teams were in some of the surrounding buildings and on the roofs of others. There was activity on the third floor, moving shadows and silhouettes could be seen.

On the north side in the dark part of the third floor a window opened, and someone yelled, "you'll never take me alive, fuckers!" Then an umbrella was seen falling from the window. Seconds later the window was bullet ridden by the roof surveillance team. Presumably, the person at the window was "Bob" or "Virgo."

The door buster crew was up front on the east side, but when they tried the door, it was unlocked. Same happened on the other two sides. This made Tolliver more nervous. It was like Virgo wanted them to go in. Tolliver thought about calling it off, but the commissioner's words rang in his head. He gave the word to proceed. It was something he would regret for the rest of his days.

Chapter 26

The first floor had a walk-in freezer and lots of wires netted around the large mostly empty room. There were four staircases and once all three teams were in the building they split up and went upstairs. As they did, the three doors they had come in through closed and locked. They continued up the stairs anyway, some perhaps out of anger, some for vengeance, and some because they were non-questioning soldiers.

Duncan Vestapoole took the first shot, right in the forehead. His brains blew all over Tim Ford and a soon to be dead Declan Reilly. Ford was in shock as he tried to get Vestapoole's brains off himself and he stared at a dead officer Reilly. Bullets seemed to be coming from everywhere and Ford knew he would not survive this. Seconds later he was dead as well.

The machine gun fire was coming from the walls and was electronically controlled. When all three teams made it to the second floor the guns began to fire. Tolliver was screaming to get out, but it was too late. Some of the Vestapoole/Ford team made it to the third floor. There were several rooms up there and one of them had a light with a track of small cardboard cut outs going back and forth and sometimes around. From the outside it looked like people were moving about on that floor in that room. Seconds after they discovered the cutouts on the tracks a faint sound of crossbow strings snapping soon morphed into the piercing of razor tipped bolts into their chests and backs.

The Holzer, Bullis team was not doing any better. Don Holzer knew his life was over when he felt the trip wire at his ankle. The spikes in the single line spike rack that hit him went through his armor and clear through his body. Others were getting hit with spike bars too. Bullis tried to get the surviving tactical team members out of there and lead them back down to the first floor. Most were now wounded as they tried to get out. There were small explosions in each corner on the first floor. The sprinkler system came on, but Bullis quickly noticed that it wasn't water. It was gasoline. Soon the whole floor erupted in flame. He tried to call his wife to say goodbye as he screamed and cried, but he was consumed by the flames along with the rest of his team.

Brad Tolliver, Mark Jenkins, Tommy Boyle, Carol Foster and others had tried to get in to save them, but it was too late. Going in would only mean dying. There was nothing they could do.

Chapter 27

The doors had to be cut open with arc welders. It was after midnight by the time the fire trucks left, and the CSI, morgue and recovery crews went in. After spending time helping Tommy Boyle convince Brad Tolliver that it wasn't his fault Jenkins left the scene. He did have someone to uncuff after all. In all 32 bodies desecrated in a variety of different ways were taken out of the warehouse. Most of those bodies were burnt beyond recognition. The cops and agents were easily identified by their badges. One of the bodies found on the third floor near the window the umbrella came out of was assumed to be the body of Virgo. The recovered umbrella was in fact a Bulgarian umbrella.

Back at her apartment Lucy York was so angry she didn't say a word to Jenkins when he walked in. He uncuffed her and she ran to the bathroom. She had been holding that pee for a long time. When the bathroom door opened, she ripped into Jenkins. He finally calmed her down and told her what happened out at the warehouse. After a while Lucy realized that Mark had saved her life. Her anger went to sadness, then she thanked Jenkins for saving her life. They talked for about an hour, she cried. Jenkins just wanted to sleep, but York had been in bed all day. She had something to eat and took a long walk through the city. When she came back, she woke up Jenkins and they talked some more. He tried to convince her to quit the force. She said she would think about it.

In the days and weeks that followed: the 32nd body was identified as Robert Culver. His picture resembled the composite that Jenkins and Boyle had worked on. Records showed that he had terminal cancer.

Jenkins, Boyle and Tolliver went to a lot of funerals. The whole city was shocked. The NYPD and the FBI were mourning their losses along with most of the city and a good part of the country. This was the largest single law enforcement disaster since 9/11/01.

The commissioner was asked to resign. Which he did and the deputy Commissioner took his place. He announced that there would be new protocols for entering buildings to make it safer for law enforcement.

The new commissioner and the mayor decided to offer Brad Tolliver a promotion to inspector. Brad was too busy mourning to consider it just yet.

The NYPD decided to wait two full weeks before closing the Virgo case just to make sure there were no more murders with the Virgo signature. After those two weeks the case was closed.

Chapter 28

Jenkins, Boyle, Tolliver and York, were sitting around the conference room at the precinct talking. Two weeks had gone by since the warehouse disaster.

Tolliver: "What a nightmare. Did Virgo lose or win?"

York: "Was it all about vengeance? And what was up with the leaves?"

Tolliver: "What could create such evil?"

Jenkins: "Evil is in all of us as is good."

Boyle: "It turns out the Robert Culver had filed complaints against the police and was harassed more for doing so. He blamed the police harassment on all his problems in life including his terminal cancer."

There was a contemplative silence and then Agent Carol Foster walked in. They all exchanged greetings and she proceeded to tell them that Jenkins had not been cleared yet, but that he could go because they, "know where to find him."

Jenkins said, "I guess I'll pack my stuff up tomorrow."

Which brought an immediate pout to York's face.

Tommy Boyle said, "We're going to miss you."

Which Brad reiterated.

Jenkins: "I'll come by and say good-bye tomorrow."

Jenkins said good-bye to Carol Foster. He was fairly sure he would not see her again. He told Boyle, Tolliver and York that he would see them the next day. Then he left the precinct. A short while later York left the conference room. Tommy could see that Brad was deeply contemplating something. This time it was something new. It wasn't the usual remorse that showed up on his face the last two weeks following the warehouse disaster.

Boyle: "You thinking about taking that Inspector job?"

Tolliver: "No, thinking about something else."

Boyle: "Care to share it?"

Tolliver: "Not yet. I need to think a little. I'll be in my office."

Brad got up and left the room leaving Tommy alone to contemplate things. Tommy started to think that since this was probably Mark's last night in town that he might want to go out and have a few beers. Then he thought, "unless Jenkins wants to bang York one more time." He decided to call Mark anyway. Jenkins answered his phone, "Hey Tommy, is everything okay? I only left a few minutes ago."

Boyle: "Yeah fine. Just wanted to know if you want to go get a few beers later being that it's your last night."

Jenkins: "Well, that sounds great, but I have a lot of packing and preparing to do."

Boyle: "I understand. Another time then.

Jenkins: "Absolutely"

Boyle: "Maybe I'll come visit you up in the wilderness."
Jenkins: "Ha. That'll be the day."
Boyle: "See you tomorrow."
Jenkins: "Yeah, I'll swing by about 9AM. See you then."

Jenkins first order of business was to swing by the Woodcalling Hotel, get what little possessions he had there, then head over to the Ritz for some relaxation and a hot bath. At the Woodcalling he had left a small bag. He disconnected the device he had put on the phone. Packed up the rest of the stuff he had there and left this poor excuse for a hotel. He took a long walk over to the East River. He picked up some rocks and pieces of concrete and put them in the bag. Then he looked around to see if there was anyone around before he dropped the bag into the river. He stood there looking across the river toward the warehouse in Queens contemplating all that had happened. He had mixed feelings, but for the most part he was just looking forward to getting back home to continue his other life or perhaps start a new one. He then took one last look in the direction of the warehouse and pivoted on one foot and started in the direction of the Ritz.

Chapter 29

Jenkins was loving his hot bath and glass of wine in the bathroom at his room in the Ritz. He could hear his phone ringing in the bedroom but did not even consider answering it. He always said, "if it's important, they will leave a message." As he sipped his wine, he thought about how great life is. Then his mind wandered, and he started thinking about making the plan to get home. As soon as the bath water started to cool, he would drain it and then take a shower. And that's exactly what he did.

He dried off put on his robe and went to check his phone while at the same time turning on his laptop. The call was from Lucy York, she wanted to get together one more time before he left town. He called her and said that would be great, but he needed to make his travel arrangements, pack and prepare for his trip. She was disappointed but very understanding. He heard the disappointment in her voice and agreed to meet her for one beer later that evening.

At the end of the workday Brad Tolliver asked Tommy Boyle to come to his office.
Tolliver: "You notice anything different about Mark?"
Boyle: "Yeah, a little. Why?"

Tolliver: "Not sure. Some of his reactions and statements after everything that went down just seems off to me."
Boyle: "What are you thinking?"
Tolliver: "I want you to go by the Woodcalling tomorrow and ask around and just see if anything seems strange to you."
Boyle: "Okay. What do you think Mark is stealing or something?"
Tolliver: "No, but like I said I feel something is *off*."
Boyle: "Alright, should I do it before he gets here or after."
Tolliver: "After."

It was just after 7PM when Lucy York showed up at the bar that Mark Jenkins had agreed to meet her at. Her dress was so sexy that Mark had trouble looking at her pretty smiling face. He knew it was a passion play and it was working. He was already thinking of changing his plans and spending a few hours with her instead of the agreed upon hour. Every guy in the bar was looking at her when she walked up to Jenkins and kissed him full on the lips. She then sat next to him at the bar and ordered a beer.
Jenkins: "I know what you're doing."
York: "What are you talking about? I'm just here to have a beer and say goodbye.
Jenkins repeated: "I know what you're doing."
York: "Is it working?"
Jenkins: "Yes."

Jenkins had gotten more done in the afternoon then he thought he would. He had his travel arrangements down and took care of a handful of other tasks. Most of his stuff was packed and waiting for him at his room in the Ritz. He knew he could spend the time with Lucy York if he wanted to, but did he want to? He always hated long goodbyes. Then he started to think that this one might feel really good.

After a few beers and many laughs they went back to York's apartment. Along the way she got many stares and even some whistles from a lot of men and some women. Jenkins couldn't disagree with how hot she looked.

At her apartment they drank a bottle of wine and made love for hours. Then they laid quietly entangled in each other until she spoke.

York: "I think I'm going to take your advice."

Jenkins: "You mean about the tantric sex?"

York: "No" she laughed.

Jenkins: "What then?"

York: "I'm going to quit."

Jenkins wondered what this meant. He hoped she didn't think that he made the suggestion so that they could be together. His road ahead could get complicated and he didn't "need no woman tagging along" as the song went.

Jenkins: "Really? I think that's great."

York: "Thanks. I never felt like I had the heart to be a cop anyway."

Jenkins: "I never thought so either. I always thought you were too nice."
York: "Awe, that's really sweet Mark."

Soon she was on him again and they made love for the last time before sleep. After she was asleep, he went to the bathroom and then got dressed and left. It was after midnight before he got back to the Ritz. He slept well and checked out. Then he went down to the precinct.

Chapter 30

Jenkins had the town car that would take him to the airport, park near the precinct. On his way to Brad's office, he saw a lot of new faces. Most likely replacements for those who had perished. There always seems to be a fresh supply, so life goes on. When he walked into Brad Tolliver's office it was exactly 9AM. Mark Jenkins was always punctual. Brad Tolliver and Tommy Boyle were there to greet him. They exchanged pleasantries and small talk. Jenkins was always uncomfortable with goodbyes. Soon he said, "Well my car is waiting so I have to go."
They all said short goodbyes and he was out the door.

On his way out the building Jenkins was thinking that Brad and Tommy seemed a little off. Maybe they were just wrapped up in saying goodbye and all the recent unpleasantness, but he thought probably not. It was something about him. Maybe they had found out that he was banging York, but he really didn't hide that. Maybe they found out he wasn't staying at the Woodcalling. But then again maybe it was something completely different. Either way he wasn't going to worry about it. He was looking forward to getting out of the city and getting out to his wilderness enclave.

As the town car went over the bridge that he would always call the Triborough, even though the official name had been changed to the

Robert F. Kennedy (RFK) Bridge, he looked back at the city. There were aspects of the city he would miss, but mostly not. He thought about Lucy York. Shortly after that he was at LaGuardia Airport.

Tommy Boyle left the precinct about 9:30 AM to go to the Woodcalling hotel. He didn't like the feeling that he was investigating a friend, but he had to agree with Brad, something did seem "off" about Jenkins. He thought maybe Jenkins felt awkward about Lucy York. Then he thought that maybe Mark was just uncomfortable with all that had taken place. Or maybe it was something completely different. Either way Tolliver had asked Boyle to check out the Woodcalling so that's what he was going to do.

The clerk at the Woodcalling seemed very eager to help one of New York's finest. It turns out that Jenkins was somewhat of a discussion point to the clerks between shifts. Also turns out that Jenkins was hardly ever there and through housekeeping they assumed he didn't even sleep there. The clerk did mention that one night there was a complaint of too much noise coming from Jenkins room and it sounded like he had a "lady friend" in there. Other than that Jenkins was a mysterious guest whom they never really saw, "Except for when he checked in a while back and when he checked out yesterday."

Boyle: "He checked out yesterday?"

Clerk: “Yes.”
Boyle: “Okay, Thanks for your help.”
Clerk: “Of course. Anytime.”

When Tommy Boyle left the Woodcalling hotel he thought he would ask York what she knew about Jenkins and where he stayed the whole time, he was in New York City. He found York in Brad’s office. She was resigning.
Boyle: “Excuse my interruption.” and he was about to turn and leave when Lucy York replied. “No, stay, I was just leaving.”
Boyle: “Can you wait a minute? I want to ask you something.”
York: “Sure, I’ll be in the conference room.”
Tommy closed the door to Brad’s office.
Boyle: “Did she just resign?”
Tolliver: “Yes. What did you find out at the Woodcalling?”
Boyle went on to tell Brad that Jenkins was hardly at the hotel and that he wanted to do some follow up questions with York. Brad agreed.

Lucy York told Tommy Boyle that although she really didn’t think her personal life was any of his business, she might answer some of his questions. She told him that she really didn’t know where Jenkins stayed. She assumed it was at the Woodcalling. Except on two nights when she admitted that he had stayed with her in her apartment. She did not feel like sharing which nights they were.

York: “Why is he in trouble?”
Boyle: “No. Brad and I just thought that something was off with him.”
York: “Something ‘off’ with Mark Jenkins? Where have you been? Have you met him? He’s definitely off!”
Boyle chuckled: “Yes, I know. But this is something else.”
York’s expression turned to one of concern. She thought it was best if she left as soon as possible. She excused herself and said she had to go because she had a lot to do.
Boyle: “Okay, well I guess this is goodbye. Brad told me you resigned.”
They hugged and York said: “Take care of yourself.”
Boyle: “Good luck in your new adventures.”
York smiled then she was gone.

Chapter 31

Mark Jenkins was finally home after a trip that he did not want to go on. He loved being in his house in the forest on the side of the mountain. The temperatures started getting colder now that Autumn had arrived, and he certainly liked that. He wrote, he played music, he took hikes in the forest and read a lot. He had tea most evenings but sometimes a Black Forest and other nights he enjoyed a good cabernet.

He had been home about two weeks when he decided to take a short trip over to Lake Placid for a couple of days. He booked himself a room at that the Crown Plaza on top of the hill behind the Olympic Center. He loved the Great Room Bar at the Crown Plaza. He'd get an Ubu and relax and look at the fantastic view. Both days he was in Lake Placid he walked around Mirror Lake. He would stop at PJ O'Neil's first. Then he would make his way around to The Cottage where he would eat something light and have another beer. He would then go on to the Dancing Bear and finally back to the Crown Plaza.

After a nap he woke up in the darkness of evening. He decided to take a ride over to Saranac Lake. When he returned, he felt a desperate need for a shower. Not only did he shower but he took a bath in the Jacuzzi tub in his room. Then he showered again.

The next day he took a short hike then walked around Mirror Lake again. He always loved Lake Placid. He stopped for a beer at each of the usual places. He had already packed up his room and placed his bag in his pickup truck. He decided to have dinner at the Adirondack Steak and Seafood company before heading home.

When he finally got on the road it was quite dark. His drive through the mountains would be less than an hour to his house. On the way he listened to NCPR on the radio like he so often did on drives through the Adirondacks. He heard on the news that two state troopers had been shot and killed near Jay Brook. The trooper's names were Fodacara and Cazzofaccia. During the newscast he pushed a CD into the player and listened to his own music for the rest of the ride home.

Chapter 32

Once again Jenkins was home enjoying tea, recording, writing, hiking, good food, good wine, good craft beer, good books, good music - some of his favorite things. It had been about a week since he returned from Lake Placid and he was just beginning to think that something was missing, and he may need a new adventure. Even if it was a short one.

Tommy Boyle called Sheriff Harrington about 9AM and told him he found out whose fingerprints were in the station wagon, but he didn't say whose. He told Harrington he was going to take a ride up the next day and surprise his old friend. He also told Harrington that Jenkins has been cleared of all charges by the FBI.

Jim Harrington hung up the phone and sat in his office looking out at the mountains in the distance. He was glad that he had gotten to do a little hiking up there in recent weeks. As he stared out at the near peak colors of Autumn, he contemplated heading out to Jenkin's place to let him know that the FBI had cleared him of all charges. He wasn't sure it was a good idea, but it was a nice day, and he would enjoy the ride.

As he left the Sot Strom cop shop, he told deputy MacDonald that he was in charge and to stay and hold the fort down. "I'm going to take a little ride."

"Okay Sheriff, have a nice ride."

Chapter 33

The Jenkins complex had a few outbuildings in the form of sheds and garages. Sheriff Harrington could see the buildings as he pulled up over the final incline and out of the woods. He realized that he had not been up to the Jenkins complex in the daytime in quite a while. He was impressed with the way Jenkins had laid it out.

Jenkins was in his study when he heard something coming up his drive. He looked out the front curtain and through the trees he could see a vehicle making its way up the mountain. He grabbed his .45 and went into the basement. He opened a door and went into a ventilated, corrugated plastic culvert. At the end of the culvert, he climbed a ladder up to a hatch in the floor of the 10x12 shed in his backyard. He waited there. On a screen he saw Harrington approaching the front door. Harrington rang the bell. No answer. Harrington went to check the garage to see if there was a vehicle in it. There were two pickup trucks in the garage. Harrington walked over to the Fridge and opened it to see if there were any Black Forests in it. Then he opened the freezer and saw a few blocks of ice. He took one out and placed it on the workbench then he brushed it off a little and looked a little deeper. Then he got some water from the sink and wiped the water on it. Then he could see that in the ice block there were tree leaves. His mind flashed back to Lucy York talking at the morning meeting they had in the precinct in NYC that morning before he traveled back to Sot Strom. She was talking about different tree leaves found by the coroner in the mouths of the victims. He snapped back to reality and unsnapped his holster and rested his right palm on the butt of his gun.

Harrington stepped outside again and started walking around the far side of the *garage. Jenkins could see Harrington* out the window of the shed now, about 50 feet away. Jenkins strapped on his left sided holster and dropped the .45 revolver into it. He cued some music on five second delay on the laptop which was connected to the outdoor Bose™ speakers. Then he stepped out of the shed to greet the sheriff.

Sheriff Harrington heard the door to the shed close and turned to see Mark walking toward him. The music started playing on the outdoor speakers "I shot the sheriff…